Pierre Lemaitre

THREE DAYS
AND A LIFE

Translated from the French by
Frank Wynne

MACLEHOSE PRESS
QUERCUS · LONDON

First published in the French language as *Trois jours et une vie* by Éditions Albin-Michel in 2016
First published in Great Britain in 2017 by MacLehose Press

This paperback edition published in 2018 by
MacLehose Press
an imprint of Quercus Publishing Ltd
Carmelite House
50 Victoria Embankment
London EC4Y 0DZ

A CIP catalogue record for this book is available
from the British Library.

ISBN (MMP) 978 0 85705 665 8
ISBN (Export MMP) 978 0 85705 809 6
ISBN (Ebook) 978 0 85705 664 1

10 9 8 7 6 5 4 3 2

Typeset in Minion by Libanus Press Ltd
Printed and bound in Great Britain by Clays Ltd, St Ives plc

For Pascaline

For my friend Camille Trumer
with my affection

1999

1

In late December 1999, an alarming series of tragic events struck Beauval, the most important of which was unquestionably the disappearance of little Rémi Desmedt. In this region of lush, dense woodland which moved to its own slow, ineluctable rhythms, the sudden disappearance of the child was met by shocked disbelief and was considered by many of the residents as a harbinger of catastrophes to come.

For Antoine, who was at the centre of the tragedy, it all began with the death of the dog Ulysses. Do not trouble to ask why its owner, Monsieur Desmedt, gave this scrawny, long-legged white-and-tan mongrel the name of a Greek hero, it will be one more mystery in this story.

The Desmedts were his next-door neighbours, and Antoine, who was twelve at the time, was all the more attached to the animal since his mother had always flatly refused to allow pets into the house; no cats, no dogs, no hamsters, nothing – they just make a mess.

Ulysses would eagerly scamper up to the fence when Antoine

called him, and often followed the gang of friends when they went to the pond or on their rambles through the surrounding woods. Whenever Antoine went out on his own, he always took Ulysses with him. He was surprised to find himself talking to the animal as to a friend. The dog would tilt his head to one side, solemn and focused, then suddenly take off, a sign that the time for talking was over.

Late summer had mostly been spent with his schoolmates building a fort in the forest on the hills of Saint-Eustache. It had been one of Antoine's ideas that, as usual, Théo had presented as his own, thereby assuming command of operations. The boy held sway over the little group because he was the tallest, and was also the mayor's son. Such things matter in a small town like Beauval (politicians who are routinely re-elected are despised, yet a mayor is treated like a king and his son like the dauphin; it is a pecking order established by traders and shopkeepers that spreads to local associations and reaches the school playgrounds by capillary action). Théo Weiser was also the dunce of his class which, in the eyes of his classmates, was proof of character. When his father gave him a hiding – as he often did – Théo would proudly flaunt his bruises, like a tribute paid by superior minds to pervasive conformism. He also turned the heads of the girls, and as a result he was feared and admired by the boys, but he was not liked. Antoine, on the other hand, asked for nothing and begrudged nothing. For him, building the fort was reward enough in itself, he did not need to be the leader.

All this changed when Kevin got a PlayStation for his

birthday. The woods around Saint-Eustache were soon deserted as everyone flocked to Kevin's house to play, something that suited Kevin's mother who would rather her son was at home than in the woods or at the pond, places she considered dangerous. Antoine's mother, however, disapproved of these Wednesday afternoons slumped on the sofa, these video games, they make you stupid, and eventually she forbade him from going. Antoine protested, not because he particularly enjoyed video games, but because he was being denied time spent with his friends. On Wednesdays and Saturdays he felt lonely.

He spent a lot of his time with the Mouchottes' daughter, Émilie, twelve years old like him. She had curly hair as blonde as a baby chick and piercing eyes, a little minx, the sort of girl it was impossible to say no to, even Théo had a crush on her, but it wasn't the same, playing with a girl.

And so Antoine went back to the woods of Saint-Eustache and began to build another fort – a tree house this time – perched three metres high in among the branches of a beech tree. He kept the project a secret, already savouring the triumph he would feel when his friends, bored with the PlayStation, would come back to the woods and discover it.

Work on the tree house took a long time. From the sawmill, he filched scraps of tarpaulin to weatherproof the windows and doors, lengths of tar paper to seal the roof, fabric to brighten the place up. He made nooks and crannies to store his treasures, the work was never-ending, especially since, having failed to come up with an overall design, he was frequently forced to change his plans. For weeks the fort took up all his time and occupied all his thoughts, which made the secret even more difficult to keep. At school he made cryptic remarks about a surprise that would have his friends' eyes popping out of their heads, but no-one took the bait. The gang was feverishly anticipating the release of the latest instalment of "Tomb Raider", they talked about nothing else.

All the time he was working on the new fort, Ulysses was Antoine's faithful canine companion. Not that he was useful, but he was there. It was his presence that gave Antoine the idea for a dog-lift that would allow Ulysses to keep him company when he was up in the tree house. He went back to the sawmills and pinched a couple of pulleys, a few metres of rope and enough timber to build a cage. The "service elevator", which was to put the finishing touch to his creation and highlight its artistry, required countless hours to complete, many of which were spent chasing Ulysses since the dog had been fearful of the prospect of being winched up ever since the first attempt. The only way to keep the lift cage horizontal was by using a fallen branch to weigh down the left-hand side. It was not an ideal solution, but eventually he managed to hoist up Ulysses. The dog whimpered pathetically as he ascended, and when Antoine clambered up to join him, he huddled against him and trembled. Antoine would close his eyes and breathe in the smell, petting the dog contentedly. The descent was much easier, since Ulysses never waited for the lift cage to reach the ground, but leaped out as soon as he felt safe to do so.

Antoine brought various tools he had found in the attic: a

pocket torch, a blanket, paper and pens for writing, everything he needed to be self-sufficient – or almost.

It should not be assumed that Antoine was by nature a loner. It was a situation temporarily forced upon him by dint of circumstance, since his mother disapproved of video games. His life was defined by the various rules and regulations issued by Madame Courtin, which were as regular as they were imaginative. A strong-willed woman, Madame Courtin had become a woman of principle since her divorce, as so many single mothers did.

Six years earlier, Antoine's father had taken advantage of a change of career to implement a change of wife. To his request for a transfer to Germany, he had appended a petition for divorce, something Blanche Courtin took as a catastrophe, which was all the more surprising as the marriage had always been a rocky one and conjugal relations had been few and far between since the birth of Antoine. From the day of his departure, Monsieur Courtin had never returned to Beauval. On birthdays and at Christmas, he would send gifts that were always at odds with his son's desires, presents for sixteen-year-olds when his son was eight, for six-year-olds when Antoine was eleven. Antoine had once visited him in Stuttgart and they had spent three long days staring stonily at each other and agreed never to repeat the experiment. Monsieur Courtin was as ill-equipped to have a son as his wife was to have a husband.

This upsetting episode brought Antoine closer to his mother. On his return from Germany, he began to interpret the slow, tedious routine of her life as evidence of her loneliness, her grief, and came to view her in a new, vaguely tragic, light. And of course, like any boy his age would have done, he came to feel responsible for his mother. Though she could be irritating (and even maddening at times), he thought he could see something in her that absolved everything, the failure and the faults, the character, the circumstances ... The idea of making his mother even more unhappy than he imagined her to be was unthinkable to Antoine. But it was a thought he would never shake.

All these things, together with the fact he was not particularly outgoing by nature, made Antoine rather a depressive child, something the sudden appearance of Kevin's PlayStation served only to reinforce. In this emotional triangle of absent father, domineering mother and distant friends, Ulysses occupied a central role.

The dog's death, and the manner in which it happened, came as a brutal shock to Antoine.

Ulysses' master, Monsieur Desmedt, was a quiet, quick-tempered man; he was solid as an oak tree, with bushy eyebrows and the face of a furious samurai, always convinced he was in the right, the type of man who does not easily change his mind. And a brawler. The only job he had ever had was as a labourer at "Weiser: Wooden Toys since 1921", the principal employer in Beauval, where his career had been punctuated by quarrels and fights. In fact he had been suspended two years earlier for having punched his foreman, Monsieur Mouchotte, in front of the staff.

He had a fifteen-year-old daughter, Valentine, who worked as a trainee hairdresser in Saint-Hilaire, and a six-year-old son,

Rémi, who worshipped Antoine and trailed around after him whenever he was allowed.

Little Rémi, it must be said, was not a burden. A chip off the old block, he already had the body of a future lumberjack and could effortlessly make the climb up to Saint-Eustache with Antoine, even going as far as the pond. Madame Desmedt considered Antoine a sensible boy – quite rightly – and one she could trust to look after Rémi when necessary. Besides, the little boy was given considerable freedom of movement. Beauval was a small town where everyone in the neighbourhood knew everyone else. Whether children were playing near the sawmills, tramping through the forest or horsing around up by Marmont or Fuzelières, there would always be an adult working nearby to keep an eye on them.

Antoine, who was finding it difficult to keep his secret, took Rémi one day to see his aerial fort. The child had been awed by Antoine's technical ability, and with great excitement had made several trips in the rudimentary lift. After which the solemn conversation: Listen to me, Rémi, this is a secret, no-one can know about the fort until it's completely finished, get it? I can trust you, can't I? Rémi promised, he swore, cross my heart and hope to die, and as far as Antoine knew he kept his promise. To Rémi, sharing a secret with Antoine meant playing with the big boys, it meant *being* a big boy. He proved himself worthy of Antoine's trust.

December 22 was mild, with temperatures several degrees warmer than the seasonal average. Though Antoine was excited by the prospect of Christmas (he hoped that his father might actually read his letter for once and send him a PlayStation), he had felt a little lonelier than usual.

Unable to bear it any longer, he had confided in Émilie.

Antoine had discovered masturbation a year earlier and now practised several times a day. Often, when out in the woods, he would lean against a tree, his jeans pooled around his ankles, and play with himself while thinking about Émilie. He had come to the realisation that it was for her that he had done all this work; he had built a nest he wanted to share with her.

Some days before the death of Ulysses, she had gone into the woods with him and studied the construction incredulously. He expected her to climb all the way up there? Being little interested in feats of civil engineering, Émilie had come intending to flirt with Antoine, but this was something she could not imagine doing three metres off the ground. She had simpered for a while, twisting a lock of blonde hair around her finger, but when Antoine became irritated by her reaction and refused to play along, she stalked off.

Émilie's visit had left Antoine with a bad taste in his mouth; she would tell the others, he felt faintly ridiculous.

Coming home from Saint-Eustache, even the holiday atmosphere and the prospect of his present could not make him forget his fiasco with Émilie which, the more he thought about it, began to feel like a humiliation.

It is true that the festivities in Beauval were tinged with a nagging uneasiness. Christmas lights, a tree in the town square, the choral society concert – as it did every year, the town had thrown itself into the holiday season, but with a certain reluctance since the threat to close the Weiser factory cast a shadow over everyone in the town. It had long been clear that the public had lost interest in traditional wooden toys. Workers were slaving to make puppets, spinning tops and little trains carved from ash wood, but they gave their own children video-game consoles – it was obvious that something was not right, that their future was in jeopardy. Rumours of a fall-off in production at Weiser circulated regularly. Already, the staff had been cut from seventy to sixty-five, then to sixty, then fifty-two. Monsieur Mouchotte, the foreman, had been laid off two years earlier and still had not found work. Even Monsieur Desmedt, among the longest-serving members of staff, was worried. He was terrified of finding his name on the next list of redundancies which some people claimed would come just after the holidays . . .

That day, shortly before 6.00 p.m., Ulysses was crossing the main road by the Beauval pharmacy when he was hit by a car. The driver did not stop.

The dog was carried to the Desmedts' house. The news spread. Antoine raced over. Lying in the garden, Ulysses was struggling to breathe. He turned his muzzle towards Antoine who stood pressed against the garden fence, petrified. One paw was clearly broken and perhaps a few ribs, someone needed to call the vet. Hands in his pockets, Monsieur Desmedt stared at his dog for a long time, then disappeared into his house, emerged with a shotgun and shot the dog at point-blank range. He then bundled the body of the dog into a grey plastic rubble sack. All sorted.

It had all happened so quickly that Antoine just stood there, mouth gaping, unable to utter a word. It hardly mattered since there was no-one to hear him. Monsieur Desmedt had already gone back into his house and closed the door. The grey sack containing Ulysses' remains had been stacked at the end of the garden with the sacks full of plaster and bricks from the shed Monsieur Desmedt had demolished a week earlier in order to build a new one.

Antoine stumbled home, devastated.

His grief was so terrible that he could not even summon the strength to tell his mother, who had heard nothing about the accident. His throat tight, a terrible heaviness weighing on his heart, he could not stop replaying the scene, the shotgun, Ulysses' head, his plaintive eyes, the hulking figure of Monsieur Desmedt . . . Unable to speak, unable to eat, he pretended he felt ill and went up to his room where he sobbed for hours. From downstairs his mother called, "Are you O.K., Antoine?" He was surprised that he managed to pronounce the words, "I'm O.K., I'm fine," convincingly enough to reassure Madame Courtin. He did not fall asleep until the small hours, and his fitful sleep was troubled by dead dogs and shotguns. He woke shattered and exhausted.

On Thursdays, Madame Courtin always left early to work at the market. Of all the odd jobs she managed to pick up through-out the year, this was the only one she truly despised. Because of Monsieur Kowalski. A tight-arse, she called him, who paid his employees the minimum wage, always late, and gave them a 50 per cent discount on food that was fit only to be thrown out. Getting up at the crack of dawn to be paid peanuts! All the same, she had been doing the job for almost fifteen years. A sense of duty. She would complain about it the night before, it made her ill. Tall and lean, angular of face, hollow-cheeked, thin-lipped, wild-eyed and skittish as a cat, Monsieur Kowalski did not conform to the stereotypical image of a butcher. Antoine, who often bumped into him, thought he was as ugly as sin. Monsieur Kowalski had bought a little charcuterie in Marmont which he now ran with the help of two assistants, his wife having died two years after he moved to the area. "Never wants to hire anyone," Madame Courtin would complain, "Thinks we're overstaffed as it is." He had a stall in Marmont market, and every Thursday he would make a tour of the neighbouring villages, ending up in Beauval. Monsieur Kowalski's long, gaunt face was the subject of ridicule among local children, who nicknamed him Frankenstein.

This Thursday she took the first bus to Marmont, as she did every week. Antoine, unable to get back to sleep, heard her quietly closing the front door. He got out of bed and from his window looked down on Monsieur Desmedt's garden. There, in a corner that was just out of sight, was the rubble sack and . . .

Once again he found himself overwhelmed by tears. Ulysses was not the only reason he was inconsolable; the dog's death was a painful echo of the loneliness he had experienced these past months, of a whole series of let-downs and disappointments.

Since his mother never came home before early afternoon,

she wrote a list of chores for him on the big slate that hung in the kitchen. There was always housework to be done, messages to be fetched, groceries to be bought from the minimart, and a whole litany of exhortations: tidy your room, there's ham in the fridge, eat a yoghurt and a piece of fruit . . .

Madame Courtin, who planned everything in advance, could always find things for him to do, she was never at a loss. For more than a week Antoine had been taking surreptitious peeks in the wardrobe at the present his father had sent, a parcel about the right size for a PlayStation, but today his heart was not in it. He was haunted by the death of the dog, by the sudden brutal manner in which it had occurred. He set to work. He did the shopping without exchanging a word with anyone, at the boulangerie he simply gave a curt nod, he could not have said a thing.

By early afternoon, his only thought was to escape to Saint-Eustache.

He packed up the lunch he had not eaten to dump it somewhere along the way. As he passed the Desmedts' house, he forced himself not to glance towards the corner of the garden where the rubbish sacks were stacked, he walked faster, his heart hammering fit to burst, being so close heightened his grief. He balled his fists and began to run and did not stop until he came to the foot of the tree house. When he had caught his breath, he looked up. The fort that had taken so many hours of work seemed grotesquely ugly now. The patchwork of tarpaulin, fabric and tar paper made it look like something from a shantytown. He remembered Émilie's rather peeved reaction when she saw it . . . Furious, he shinned up the tree and set about destroying everything, hurling planks and pieces of timber as far as he could. When the debris had been scattered, he climbed down again, panting for breath. He leaned against the tree, slumped to the ground, and sat there for a long time, wondering what to do. He had lost all interest in life.

He missed Ulysses.

But it was Rémi who showed up.

Antoine saw the little boy in the distance. He was walking carefully, as though afraid to trample the mushrooms. Eventually he reached Antoine, whose body was racked by sobs. The child stood there looking helpless. He peered up into the tree, saw that everything had been wrecked, opened his mouth to speak only to be brutally interrupted.

"Why did your dad have to do it?" Antoine screamed, "Why did he do it, WHY?"

Rage had him leaping to his feet. Rémi stared at him, his eyes wide, and listened to this diatribe he did not understand since, at home, he had simply been told that Ulysses had run off – something the dog often did.

In that moment, consumed by an overwhelming feeling of injustice, Antoine was no longer himself. The boundless anguish he felt at Ulysses' death was transformed into anger. In a blind fury, he grabbed the branch he had used to steady the lift cage, brandishing it as though Rémi were a dog and he the master.

Rémi, who had never seen Antoine in such a rage, was terrified.

He turned, took a step.

Antoine gripped the branch in both hands and, wild with rage, lashed out at the child. The blow caught him on the right temple. Rémi crumpled to the ground. Antoine went to him, reached out and shook the boy's shoulder.

Rémi?

He must be stunned.

Antoine rolled him over so he could tap the boy's cheeks, but once on his back he saw Rémi's eyes were open.

Fixed, glassy.

And a simple truth dawned on him: Rémi was dead.

2

The branch has just fallen from his hands. He looks down at the child's sprawled body. There is something strange about the posture that Antoine cannot quite place, a helplessness . . . What have I done? And what do I do now? Go and get help? No, he can't just leave the boy here, he has to carry him, to pick him up and run all the way to Beauval, run straight to Docteur Dieulafoy.

"Don't worry," Antoine whispers. "We'll get you to hospital."

His voice is almost inaudible, as though he is talking to himself.

He bends, slips his arms under the boy's body and gathers him up. He does not know his own strength, which is just as well because there is a long road ahead . . .

Antoine begins to run, but Rémi's body suddenly feels like a terrible weight in his arms. He stops. No, it's not that Rémi is heavy, but that he is limp. The head is thrown back, the arms hang by his sides, the feet jiggle as though he were a puppet. It is like carrying a sack.

Antoine's willpower suddenly fails, his knees buckle as he is forced to set Rémi back down on the ground.

Can he really be . . . dead?

Faced with this question, Antoine's mind goes blank. It requires an almost superhuman effort to hunker down next to the boy. He studies the pallor of the skin, the parted lips . . . He reaches out, but he cannot touch the child's face. There is an invisible barrier between them, his hand encounters an immovable obstacle that prevents it advancing further.

The consequences begin to dawn on Antoine.

He has scrabbled to his feet and is pacing nervously, sobbing, he can no longer bring himself to look at Rémi's body. Fists clenched, his mind white-hot, his every muscle tensed, he paces up and down, what should he do, tears come so fast he can barely see, he wipes them away with his sleeve.

And then he feels a surge of hope – he moved!

Antoine feels like calling on the forest as witness: he just moved, didn't he? Did you see that? He bends down.

But now, not the slightest tremor, nothing.

Except that the place where the branch made contact has changed colour, it is now a deep red, a huge bruise that covers the boy's whole cheek, and seems to spread like a wine stain on a white table cloth.

He needs to make sure, to check whether the child is breathing. It is something he once saw on T.V., they put a mirror to someone's lips to see whether the glass misted. But he has no chance of finding a mirror here . . .

There is nothing else to do. Antoine tries to concentrate,

he crouches over the body, brings his ear close to the boy's mouth, but the rustle of the forest and his hammering heart make it impossible to hear anything.

He needs to try something different. Antoine opens his eyes wide and, fingers splayed, he reaches his hand out towards Rémi's chest, towards his Fruit of the Loom T-shirt. As he touches the fabric, he feels a wave of relief: it is warm. He's alive! He places his hand firmly on the child stomach. Where is the heart? He feels for his own heart. It is further up, further to the left, it is not at all where he thought . . . And as he fumbles for a pulse he almost forgets what he is doing. There: his left hand has found his own heart, his right is pressed to the same spot on Rémi's chest. Beneath one hand he feels a powerful throb, beneath the other, nothing. He presses a little harder, feels around, still nothing; he places both his hands flat on the child's chest, there is no pulse. The heart is dead.

Antoine cannot help himself, he lashes out. He slaps the child hard, once, twice. Why did you die? Why did you have to die?

The boy's head lolls from side to side. Antoine stops abruptly. What the hell is he doing! Slapping Rémi . . . who is dead.

He scrabbles to his feet again, distraught.

What should he do? Over and over he asks himself the same question, his thoughts refuse to budge.

He begins to circle the body again, wringing his hands, savagely brushing away an endless torrent of tears.

He has to give himself up. To the police. What would he say?

I was playing with Rémi, I hit him with a branch and killed him?

Besides, how can he confess, the nearest police station is in Marmont, eight kilometres from Beauval . . . His mother would find out from the *gendarmes*. The news would kill her, she couldn't bear to be the mother of a murderer. And his father, how would he react? He would send another present . . .

Antoine is in prison. Forced to share a tiny cell with three older, vicious boys. They look like characters from the T.V. series "Oz" – he watched a few episodes on the sly – there is this one guy, a terrifying thug named Vernon Schillinger, who has a thing for pretty boys. If he goes to prison, Antoine is convinced he will come face to face with someone like that.

And who would come to visit? Images flash past, his friends, Émilie, Théo, Kevin, the school headmaster . . . Suddenly the image of Monsieur Desmedt rears up, the hulking frame, the blue overalls, the square jaw, the grey eyes.

No, Antoine will not have to go to prison, there will not be time, when Monsieur Desmedt finds out what happened he will kill him, just like he killed his dog, a shotgun blast to the belly.

He looks at his watch: 2.30 p.m., the sun is high, Antoine is bathed in sweat.

He needs to make a decision, but something tells him it has already been made: he will go home, say nothing, go and hole up in his room as though he had never been out, how will anyone know it was him? No-one will notice Rémi is missing until . . . He tries to calculate, but gets confused, he tries counting on his fingers, but counting what? How long will it take for Rémi to be found? Hours, days? And in any case, Rémi has often been seen hanging out with Antoine and his friends, they are bound to be questioned . . . The others are probably all at Kevin's house right now, playing on the PlayStation, leaving only him, Antoine, which means everyone will suspect him.

No, what he needs to do is make sure that Rémi is never found.

The image of the rubbish sack containing the body of Ulysses flashes through his mind.

Get rid of him.

Rémi disappears, no-one knows where he went, there, that's the solution, they'll search for him and no-one will even imagine that . . .

Antoine is still pacing up and down next to the body, he cannot bring himself to look at it. It freaks him out, makes it impossible to think.

What if Rémi told his mother he was going up to Saint-Eustache to see Antoine?

People might be out looking for him already, any minute now he will hear voices calling, "Rémi! Antoine!"

Antoine feels the trap snap shut. His tears begin to well once more. He is done for.

He needs to hide the body, but where? How? If he hadn't destroyed the tree house, he could have winched Rémi up in the lift, no-one would think to look for him up there. The crows would have feasted on him.

He is overcome by the sheer scale of the tragedy. In a few

fleeting seconds, his whole life has changed course. He is a murderer.

These two thoughts seem irreconcilable, surely it is impossible to be twelve years old and a murderer . . .

Desperation rises in him like a flood tide.

Time passes, still Antoine does not know what to do. By now, back in Beauval, people are probably starting to worry.

The millpond! It will look as though he drowned!

No, the body would float. Antoine has nothing to weigh it down. When the child is fished out, someone will notice the bruise on his temple. Maybe they will think he fell and hit his head?

Antoine is at a complete loss.

The beech tree! Antoine can picture it as though it were right in front of him. A huge tree that toppled years ago. One day, without warning, it simply keeled over, like an old man dropping dead, and disinterred a huge knot of roots, a vast bank of earth as tall as a man. It brought down other trees with it as it fell, creating a tangle of branches where he and his friends used to play a long time ago until, for no particular reason, they grew bored of the place . . . The beech tree collapsed onto a sort of burrow, a cavernous hole that no-one dared climb down into – even before the tree fell – no-one knows where it leads, or whether it leads anywhere, but Antoine can think of no other solution.

He has made his decision, he turns around.

Rémi's face has changed again, it is grey now, the bruise has blossomed and grown darker. The mouth is gaping. Antoine feels queasy. He will never have the strength to go all that way, to the far side of Saint-Eustache, even under normal circumstances it would take fifteen minutes.

He did not think he had any tears left. They stream down his face, drip from his chin. He blows his nose into his hand and wipes it on some leaves, approaches the body of the child, hunkers down and grabs the wrists. They are thin, warm, soft, like sleeping animals.

Turning his head away, Antoine begins to drag . . .

He has not gone six metres before he encounters obstacles, tree stumps, undergrowth. The forest of Saint-Eustache has not been private land for as long as anyone can remember, it is a dense snarl of thickets, closely spaced trees, many collapsing onto one another, and brambles and coppices; dragging the body is impossible, he will have to carry it.

Antoine cannot decide.

All around him the forest cracks like the beams of an old ship. He shifts his weight from one foot to the other. How can he summon up the courage?

He does not know where the surge of strength comes from, but brusquely he bends down, grabs Rémi and slings the boy over his shoulder. And he sets off, walking quickly, skirting those tree trunks he cannot step over.

He stumbles, his foot catching on a root, trips over and falls, Rémi's body lands on top of him, a heavy jumble of floppy, flailing limbs twisting around at him like an octopus, Antoine lets out a scream and pushes the corpse away, struggles to his feet still screaming and backs against a tree, panting for breath . . . He had always assumed a corpse was stiff, he has seen pictures, dead people stiff as planks. This one, on the other hand, is limp, as though boneless.

Antoine tries to steel himself. Come on, you've got to hide the body, make it disappear, once you've done that everything will be fine. He takes a step closer, squeezes his eyes shut, grabs Rémi's arms, bends so he can hoist the boy onto his shoulders again, and sets off once more, treading carefully. Carrying Rémi on his back makes him feel like a firefighter saving someone from a burning building. Like Peter Parker when he carries Mary Jane.

The temperature has dropped, but still he is dripping with sweat. And exhausted; his feet seem to weigh a tonne, his shoulders have begun to sag. But he has to move faster, people back in Beauval will be worrying.

And his mother will be home soon.

And Madame Desmedt will call round to ask her whether she has seen Rémi.

And when he gets home, she will ask him the same question, and he will say, Rémi? No, I haven't seen him, I was . . .

Where was he?

As he clambers over fallen branches, circumvents the dense thickets, stumbles over saplings and the occasional root snaking above the ground, staggering under the weight of the dead child, he tries to work out where he would have been if he had not been here, but he can think of nothing. "The boy's not got much imagination . . ." his teacher had said last year before he started his last year in primary school. Monsieur

Sánchez has never really liked him, he had time only for Adrien, who had always been teacher's pet, there have even been rumours about Monsieur Sánchez and Adrien's mother . . . This is a woman who always wears perfume – not at all like Antoine's mother – at the school gates, everyone stares at her because she smokes in the street and wears . . .

It was bound to happen, for a second time he falls flat on his face, bangs his head against a tree trunk, releases his burden and howls as he sees Rémi tumble over him and hit the ground with a sickening thud. Instinctively, he had reached out . . . For a moment, he had worried that Rémi might be hurt, had thought about him as though he were still alive.

He can see the boy's back, his skinny legs, his little hands, it is heartbreaking.

Antoine cannot bear it any more. He lies there, sprawled among the leaves, breathing in the earthy smell the way he once breathed in the smell of Ulysses' fur. He is so tired he wishes he could sleep here, wishes he could sink into the earth, wishes he too might die.

He will give up, he does not have the strength.

He glances at his watch, his mother must be home by now. It is difficult to explain, but if he manages to get to his feet again, it will be for her sake. She has done nothing to deserve this. It would kill her. He will have killed her, if she finds out that . . .

Painfully, he stands up. Rémi has scratches on his arm and on his legs, Antoine cannot help but imagine that they must hurt, it's crazy, he cannot get it into his head that Rémi is dead, he simply cannot admit it. It is not a corpse but the boy he knows that he heaves onto his shoulders and carries through the forests of Saint-Eustache, the boy he hoisted in the lift cage with Ulysses, the boy who screamed *yaaaay!* He loved the lift.

Antoine is beginning to hallucinate.

As he moves forward, taking long strides, he sees Rémi coming towards him, sees him up ahead, smiling and waving at him, *hiya!*, he always admired Antoine. Hey, is that a tree house? He looks up into the branches, he sees a small boy with a chubby face and twinkling eyes, he's very well spoken for his age, alright, he's a kid, he thinks like a kid, but he's interesting, he asks amazing questions . . .

Antoine did not realise how close he was. He has made it.

There it is. The huge, fallen beech tree.

To reach the trunk and the burrow beneath it, he will have to fight his way through thick brambles and, to make things more difficult, it is much darker in this part of the woods.

Antoine is no longer thinking, he moves forward. Several times he loses his balance and grabs for whatever he can, almost falls, rips his shirtsleeve, but he forges on, Rémi's head bangs against a tree with a dull thud . . . Twice, the boy's arms get caught on thorns and Antoine has to tug them free.

Finally, after a fierce battle, he is ready to set to work.

Two metres away, beneath the thick beech trunk, is the gaping maw of the burrow. Like a cave. To reach it he has to negotiate a steep mound of earth.

Antoine gently sets the body at his feet, crouches and begins to roll it. Like a carpet.

The child's head bumps and bangs, Antoine squeezes his

eyes shut and keeps pushing. When he opens them again, he is halfway up the slope. He is frightened by the yawning crevasse, like the entrance to a furnace. The mouth of an ogre. No-one knows what is inside, whether it is deep, nor what exactly made this chasm. Antoine always assumed it had been left by another tree uprooted when the great beech fell.

There. He has made it.

Antoine does not feel reassured by this fact. Remi's little body lies at his feet, on the edge of the crevasse, the vast beech trunk louring above them both.

Now the time has come to push him in, Antoine cannot bring himself to do it.

He clutches his head in both hands and howls in pain. Wild with grief, he leans against the fallen trunk, slides his right foot beneath the child's hip and gently lifts it.

He turns his face towards the sky and gives a swift kick.

The body rolls slowly, at the very edge of the crevasse it seems to hesitate then, suddenly, it tips and drops away.

The last image burned onto Antoine's memory is of Rémi's arm, of his little hand seeming to clutch at the soil, trying to stop himself falling.

Antoine stands, rooted to the spot.

The body has disappeared. Struck by a nagging doubt, he kneels, stretches out his arm, fearfully at first, plunges it into the crevasse and gropes around.

He can feel nothing.

He gets to his feet, dazed. There is nothing now. No Rémi, nothing, everything has disappeared.

Nothing but the image of that tiny hand with its curled fingers slowly disappearing ...

Antoine turns and, with a giant stride, mechanically steps over the brambles.

When he comes to the edge of the bank, he hurtles down the hill, he runs, he runs, he runs.

The shortest route home means having to cross the road twice. Antoine crouches in a thicket beside a bend in the road that makes it impossible to see any approaching traffic, he listens intently but can hear nothing above his pounding heart ...

He stands, glances quickly to the left and right, then goes for it. He dashes across the road and is diving back into thick woodland just as Monsieur Kowalski's delivery van appears.

Antoine throws himself into the ditch and freezes. The van roars past.

Antoine does not wait, he sets off again at a run. Three hundred metres from the town he pauses for a moment in a copse, but he knows he has no time to think, he must decide, and quickly. He emerges from the woods and walks on in what he hopes is a poised manner; he catches his breath.

Does he look normal? He runs his fingers through his hair. There are a few scratches on his hands, nothing too obvious, he hurriedly brushes the dirt and the twigs clinging to his shirt, his trousers ...

He had thought he would be afraid to go home, but no, on the contrary, the boulangerie, the grocer's, the gates of the *mairie*, the familiar landmarks make the nightmare seem remote, they welcome him back to everyday life.

To hide the tear in his shirtsleeve, he fumbles for the cuff and grips it in his clenched fist.

He looks down.

He has lost his wristwatch.

3

It was a diver's watch with a black dial, a fluorescent green strap and an impressive number of functions: a tachymeter, a bezel with notches indicating time zones around the world, a stopwatch, a calculator . . . It was a big watch, much too big for Antoine's wrist, but that was precisely what he liked about it. He had had to nag his mother for months to get permission to buy it, and even then she conceded only in exchange for a long list of additional commitments and chores and after a lengthy sermon about the concepts of thrift, necessity, futility, deferred gratification and various other notions that were obscure to him but which his mother had read about in magazine articles dealing with childhood and education.

How would he explain the sudden disappearance of the watch? Because his mother would be sure to notice and ask about it, she had an unerring eye for such things.

Should he retrace his steps? Where could he have lost it? Maybe it had fallen into the crevasse beneath the giant beech tree . . . But what if he had lost it on his way back . . . ? Maybe even on the road? If it was found, might it not lead the search party straight to him? Worse still, it might be used as evidence against him.

Preoccupied by these questions, Antoine did not immediately notice the unusual commotion in the Desmedts' garden.

A certain restiveness was agitating a group of six or seven people, most of them women: the grocer, who was scarcely ever in her shop, Madame Kernevel, Claudine, and even old Madame Antonetti – so thin she was literally fading away, who trembled as she turned her beady witch's eyes on you and who was vicious as a stoat, to boot.

This gaggle of women hid the figure of Madame Desmedt, whose voice could be heard only faintly – a somewhat nasal drawl. She seemed to have a head cold from one end of the year to the other. "Hayfever," she would insist knowledgeably, "I'm allergic to the dust from the sawmills. Not much I can do about it living round here, now is there . . . ?" And she would let her arms fall and slap against her thighs to show what a martyr she was to her suffering.

When he saw the commotion in the garden, Antoine slowed his pace. He heard hurried footsteps behind him; it was Émilie. She was about to draw alongside him, panting and out of breath, when a voice shouted:

"There he is, there's Antoine!"

Elbowing her way through the scrum, Madame Desmedt emerged from the garden clutching a handkerchief and ran towards him. The whole group raced after her.

"Do you know where Rémi is?" she said breathlessly.

In that split second, he knew he would not be able to lie. His throat tight, he shook his head. No . . .

"But . . ." Madame Desmedt said.

This single syllable, uttered as a strangled cry, was filled with such pain that Antoine almost burst into tears. It was only thanks to the grocer's intervention that he managed to hold back:

"So he wasn't with you?"

Antoine swallowed hard and looked around. His eyes fell on Émilie, frozen in her tracks watching the scene intently. He managed to say in a low voice:

"No . . ."

He was on the verge of collapse when the grocer said:

"Where did you see him last?"

He was about to say that he hadn't see Rémi all day. The blood drained from his face and he nodded vaguely towards the garden. The clamour of chattering voices started up again.

"For God's sake," the grocer snapped, "the child can't have vanished into thin air!"

"If he went through the town someone would have seen him . . ."

"Maybe, maybe not . . ."

Madame Desmedt was still staring at Antoine, but she seemed to be looking straight through him, coming to terms with what was happening. Her bottom lip trembled, her eyes were blank. Her agony was like a knife in Antoine's heart.

He turned slowly and, without even looking at Émilie, set off towards his own house.

Before he opened his front door, he turned. Madame

Desmedt looked to him like Monsieur Préville's wife, who sometimes managed to give her home nurse the slip only to be found in the middle of the road, eyes wild, howling for her only daughter who had been dead for more than fifteen years. Next to her grief, her anguish, the blonde, fresh-faced figure of Émilie made a terrible contrast.

As he stepped inside the house, Antoine felt a rush of relief. In the sitting room, the Christmas tree glittered and twinkled like a neon sign.

He had lied and they had believed him. But was he out of the woods?

And what about his watch . . .

His mother was not home yet, but she would not be long. He went up to his bedroom, pulled off his shirt, rolled it into a ball and stuffed it under the mattress. He pulled on a clean T-shirt as he walked over to the window and cautiously parted the curtains to watch the lumbering figure of Monsieur Desmedt coming home from the factory, heading towards the garden where the little group was still gathered. He radiated such power, such brutality, that Antoine took a step back . . . The very thought of having to face the man made his stomach churn. He suddenly felt sick. He clapped his hand over his mouth and just had time to dash to the toilet and lean over the bowl . . .

Sooner or later, they would find Rémi's body and they would come back to question him.

He stumbled back to his bedroom, his legs gave out and he fell to his knees.

In less than an hour, maybe, if they found his wristwatch on the path, if they realised that he had lied.

A detachment of police officers would surround the house to make sure he did not escape. Three, maybe four of them would slip into the house. Armed to the teeth, they could creep up the stairs, hugging the walls, while outside an officer with a megaphone would bark orders for him to surrender, to come out with his hands up . . . There would be nothing he could do. They would clap him in handcuffs. "We know you murdered Rémi! Where did you hide the body?"

Perhaps they would cover his head with a jacket to spare him the humiliation. He would be dragged down the stairs, past his grief-stricken mother sobbing "Antoine, Antoine, Antoine . . ." Out in the street, the whole town would be waiting, there would be shouts, screams, bastard, murderer, child-killer! The *gendarmes* would bundle him into a police van, but just at that moment Monsieur Desmedt would loom up and whip the jacket from his head so that Antoine could see him grip the gun at his hip and fire.

Antoine felt a piercing pain in his belly, he felt a desperate urge to go back to the toilet but stayed kneeling on the bedroom floor, rooted to the spot with fear by the sound of his mother's voice:

"Antoine, are you home?"

Quick, throw her off the scent.

He struggled to his feet and went to sit at his desk.

His mother was already standing in the doorway.

"What's going on? What's all the fuss over at Bernadette's?"

He gave a feeble shrug, how would I know?

But he had talked to Madame Desmedt, he could not pretend he did not know what was happening.

"It's Rémi . . . they're looking for him."

"Really? They don't know where he is?"

This was so like his mother.

"If they're looking for him, obviously they don't know where he is, Maman, or they wouldn't be looking."

But Madame Courtin was not listening, she had stepped into the room and moved to the window. Antoine stood behind her.

More people had gathered in the garden now that Monsieur Desmedt had arrived, friends from the bar, his workmates from Weiser. Steel-grey clouds scudded across the overcast sky. In this twilight glow, the group clustered around Monsieur Desmedt looked like a baying mob. He felt a shudder run through him.

"Are you cold?" his mother said.

Antoine gave an exasperated shrug.

Down below, all eyes turned to the mayor as he strode into the garden. Madame Courtin opened the window.

"Wait up, wait up," said Monsieur Weiser, who had a tendency to repeat himself.

He was holding an outspread hand up to Monsieur Desmedt's chest.

"You don't just go bothering the *gendarmes* like that!"

"What do you mean, 'like that'?" roared Monsieur Desmedt. "So my missing son is nothing, as far as you're concerned?"

"Missing, missing . . ."

"I suppose you know where he is, do you? A six-year-old boy that no-one's seen for . . ." – he checked his watch, frowning as he made a quick calculation – "nigh on three hours. Does that not count as missing in your book?"

"Right, so where was he last seen, this child?" Monsieur Weiser said, manifestly attempting to be helpful.

"He walked his father part of the way back to his work, didn't he, Roger?" Madame Desmedt said, her voice quavering.

Monsieur Desmedt gave a curt nod. He always came home for lunch at noon and, when he set off for work again, Rémi would usually walk a little way with him, then turn and trot back home.

"So where were you, then, when he turned back?" asked the mayor.

Monsieur Desmedt seemed not best pleased to have the owner of the factory where he worked setting himself up as judge and jury. Next thing you know he would be telling him how to raise his family. There was a barely concealed fury in his response.

"Don't you think maybe it's the *gendarmes* that should be doing this job, not you?"

He was a head taller than the mayor and had stepped closer so that he towered over him. He was speaking in a booming voice and Monsieur Weiser had to make a visible effort not to give any ground. It was an affront to his authority and his dignity. The women had retreated, the men had stepped closer, he was more or less surrounded: they were all workers, or fathers or brothers of the workers at Monsieur Weiser's factory.

This unexpected confrontation rekindled the fear of unemployment that was weighing heavily on them. It was difficult to tell whether Monsieur Desmedt's anger stemmed from his role as Rémi's father, or as Weiser's employee.

Unmoved by the clash between Monsieur Desmedt and the mayor of Beauval, Madame Kernevel had decided to take the initiative, she had gone back to her house and picked up the telephone.

The arrival of the *gendarmes* was more than Madame Courtin could bear. She rushed outside.

Other neighbours began to appear, passers-by stopped to listen, the absent were summoned, and those who could not squeeze into the Desmedts' garden stood gathered in the street, a milling crowd chattering and calling to each other, though their voices were low, a whispered susurration that sounded grave and anxious.

Antoine stared, spellbound, at the police van.

It often drove through the town and everyone knew the *gendarmes* by sight; they would call in to the café, ostentatiously order only non-alcoholic drinks and insist on paying. They would occasionally get involved in altercations, or deliver a summons; their arrival was invariably something of an event, the townspeople would wonder who it concerned and, if the van stopped nearby, would stroll over to see.

Antoine, who knew nothing about ranks, thought the senior officer looked very young. He felt curiously relieved.

The three officers parted the crowd and went into the garden.

The senior officer briefly questioned Madame Desmedt. As he listened to her answers, he took her by the arm and steered her back towards the house. Monsieur Desmedt trailed behind, turning to glower at the mayor who had tried to follow the group.

Then they disappeared. The door closed behind them.

The crowd split into various smaller groups according to their affinities: workers at the Weiser factory, neighbours who knew each other, parents of schoolchildren. No-one made a move to leave.

Antoine noticed that the atmosphere had changed. The arrival of the forces of law and order had elevated a minor occurrence to the status of an event. This was no longer an isolated incident, but something that concerned the whole town. Antoine could sense it. The low, serious voices, the anxious questions – it seemed to him, given that he was involved, that things were taking an ominous turn.

He hurriedly closed the window and raced back to the toilet. He sat on the seat, his body bent double, but nothing would come. His stomach heaved, racked by painful spasms. He braced his arms . . . and then he heard a noise.

The pain subsided instantly, he looked up. He thought about a stag he had once seen in the woods, how he had watched it rear, turning its head from side to side, cocking its ears to hear what it could not see; sensing Antoine's presence it had straightaway adopted the skittish, nervous demeanour of a hunted animal . . .

Antoine now realised that his mother was not alone, there

was a clamour of voices, men's voices. He stood up and, not stopping to buckle the belt of his jeans, ran back to his bedroom.

"I'll go and get him for you," his mother was saying, he could already hear her footsteps on the stairs.

Antoine moved as far away from the door as he could, he needed to put on a brave face, but he did not have time.

"It's the police," his mother said, coming into his room, "They want to talk to you."

She did not sound worried in the slightest. Antoine thought he could detect a hint of satisfaction in her tone: her son, and therefore she, was a "person of interest", they were being consulted, they were entitled to have a say in the matter. They were important.

"Talk to me . . . ? About what?" Antoine said.

"About Rémi, of course . . . What do you think?"

Madame Courtin was almost shocked by Antoine's questions. But both of them were caught off guard by the appearance of the *gendarme*.

"May I . . . ?"

He stepped into the room slowly but authoritatively.

Antoine could not put an age on him, but he was younger than the officer in the garden. He looked at Antoine with a confident smile and glanced at the contents of the room, came over and knelt in front of the boy. His cheeks were impeccably shaved, his eyes bright and piercing, and his ears unnaturally big.

"Listen, Antoine, you know Rémi Desmedt, don't you?"

Antoine swallowed hard and nodded in agreement. The *gendarme*'s hand reached out towards his shoulder but hovered in mid-air.

"There's no need to be afraid, Antoine . . . I just wanted to ask when you last saw him."

Antoine looked up, saw his mother standing in the doorway of his bedroom watching the scene with an air of satisfaction, almost of pride.

"You need to look at me, Antoine. You need to tell me where you last saw Rémi."

The voice had changed, it was firmer, he wanted an answer to his question . . . to which Antoine had given no thought. It had been easier dealing with Madame Desmedt. He turned to the window, trying to pluck up courage.

"In the garden," he managed to mutter, "down there, in the garden . . ."

"What time would that have been?"

Antoine took comfort in the fact that his voice had not quavered too much, no more than that of any twelve-year-old being questioned by a *gendarme*.

He racked his brain: what had he heard Madame Desmedt saying earlier?

"About half past one, something like that . . ."

"Good. And what was Rémi doing in the garden?"

He blurted the answer.

"He was looking at the sack with the dog in it."

The *gendarme* frowned. Antoine realised that without an explanation, his answer made no sense.

"It was Rémi's father. He killed their dog yesterday. He put it in a rubbish sack."

The *gendarme* smiled.

"Well, well, things certainly have been happening in Beauval . . ."

But Antoine was in no mood for jokes.

"O.K.," said the *gendarme*. "So where is it, exactly, this rubbish sack?"

"Down there," he pointed out of the window, "in the garden, with the sacks of rubble. He killed him with a shotgun, stuffed him in a rubbish bag."

"So, Rémi was in the garden, and he was looking at this rubbish sack, is that right?"

"Yes. He was crying . . ."

The *gendarme* pursed his lips: O.K., I can understand that.

"And you didn't see him after that . . ."

A shake of the head. The *gendarme* was staring at him, his lips still puckered, focusing on what he had just heard.

"And you didn't see a car stopping or anything like that . . . ?"

No.

"I mean, anything out of the ordinary?"

No.

"O.K., then!"

The *gendarme* slapped his thighs: right, back to work . . .

"Thanks, Antoine, you've been a great help."

He got to his feet. As he left, he made a little gesture to Madame Courtin who was about to follow him downstairs.

"Oh, yes, one more thing Antoine . . ."

He had stopped in the doorway and turned.

"When you saw him, down there in the garden . . . where were you heading?"

Instinctive response:

"To the pond."

Antoine realised he had answered quickly. *Too* quickly.

So he said it again, more calmly.

"I went up to the pond."

The *gendarme* nodded, the pond, O.K., alright.

4

The *gendarme* stood on the pavement, unconvinced.

He watched as the crowd in the street swelled and grew more restive.

Impatient voices offered a running commentary on what was happening. The gathering darkness made it seem less likely that Rémi would come home. What was being done? Who was in charge? The mayor shuttled between the group of workers and the police van, calming the former and quizzing the latter . . . The prospect of mass outburst could not be discounted since all those present, though for very different reasons, felt they were victims of injustice and had found in this an opportunity to express their anger.

The young *gendarme* shrugged. He snapped his fingers and beckoned his fellow officers.

Within a few minutes, an ordnance survey map had been spread out and the *gendarme* was calling for volunteers, who raised their hands like children at school. They were counted. Since Madame Desmedt had searched the town centre as soon as she noticed that Rémi had disappeared, the volunteers were each assigned an area outside the town and told to comb the roads and pathways leading into Beauval.

Engines roared into life. The men swaggered towards their cars and climbed behind steering wheels as though going on a hunting trip. Even the mayor helped out, getting into his official car so he could participate in the search. Though they were mobilising for a good cause, there was something in the atmosphere, a whiff of mob mentality, a vindictiveness, that self-righteous determination so often witnessed before a lynching.

Looking down from his window, Antoine had the paradoxical feeling that the people driving away were in fact coming for him.

The young *gendarme* did not immediately get into his car but stood thoughtfully watching this determined crowd. What had been set in motion might not be so easy to stop.

A missing person alert was issued across the *département*.

Photographs and descriptions of Rémi Desmedt were posted up in public places.

At the Desmedt house, the women of the town took turns to sit with Bernadette. In fact, once she had put away the shopping and prepared the evening meal, Madame Courtin shouted up the stairs:

"Antoine, I'm going round to see Bernadette!"

She did not wait for an answer. From his window Antoine watched her hurry across the garden.

Antoine had been very shaken by the visit from the *gendarme*.

There had been something shrewd, something mistrusting about the man . . .

He had not believed Antoine.

He was convinced of this. The way the *gendarme* had lingered for a long time on the pavement, considering what Antoine had said, thinking about going back upstairs and confronting him.

Antoine stared down at the now-deserted garden, not daring to move. As soon as he turned around, the *gendarme* would be there, in his bedroom, he would have closed the door, would be sitting on the bed and staring at him. Outside, the town would be strangely calm, as though utterly drained of its lifeblood.

For an interminable moment, the *gendarme* would say nothing and Antoine would inexorably come to realise that his very silence was a confession.

"So, you were up at the pond . . ."

Antoine nods, yes, that's right.

The *gendarme* seems saddened by this response, he purses his lips and makes tutting noises to express his disappointment.

"You know what's going to happen, Antoine?"

He gestures to the window.

"All those people will be back soon. Most of them will have found nothing, obviously, but Monsieur Desmedt will have stopped by the little path, the one that leads up to Saint-Eustache."

Antoine swallows. He does not want to hear what comes next, but the *gendarme* is determined to spare him nothing.

"He will find your wristwatch on the path, so he will keep

walking as far as the big beech tree. He will bend down, reach into the crevasse, his fingers will close around something and he'll pull – and what will come out, eh? You tell me, Antoine, what will he pull out? Little Rémi . . . Dead as a stone. His arms and legs all limp, his little head lolling the way it did when you carried him on your back, remember?"

Antoine cannot move, he opens his mouth, but nothing comes out.

"And Monsieur Desmedt will gather his son in his arms and carry him home. Picture the scene: Monsieur Desmedt walking through Beauval with his dead son in his arms, followed by everyone in the neighbourhood . . . And what do you think he'll do? He will calmly go into his house, lay Rémi in his mother's arms, reappear with his shotgun, walk across the garden, climb the stairs and come into this room . . ."

At that moment, Monsieur Desmedt bursts into the room carrying his shotgun. He is so tall he has to stoop to get through the door. The *gendarme* does not move, he stares at Antoine, I warned you, what do you expect me to do now?

Monsieur Desmedt strides forward, holding his rifle at hip level, his looming shadow blotting out Antoine, the window, and the whole town beyond . . .

A burst of gunfire.

Antoine let out a scream.

He was kneeling on the floor, clutching his belly, he had vomited a little bile.

He would give anything in the world to be anywhere but here . . . The thought gives him pause.

Anywhere but here . . .

This is what he has to do. Run away.

He looks up, shocked at the obviousness of this solution. How did he not think of it before now? This glimmering shaft of light shakes him from his torpor. His brain, which had been running in slow motion, ramps up several gears. He is excited.

He wipes his mouth with his sleeve and paces up and down his bedroom. Determined not to forget anything, he grabs his exercise book and a marker and quickly jots down everything he can think of: clothes, money, train, plane (?), Spiderman, passport!, the travel document for Germany, paper, food, tent (?), rucksack . . .

He has to move fast. Leave this evening, tonight.

By tomorrow morning, if he went about it the right way, he would be far away.

He dismissed the idea of secretly going to see Émilie to say goodbye, she would be bound to tell people. Better that she find out tomorrow morning that Antoine has left for parts unknown, that she will never hear from him again – no, wait – he would send her postcards from all around the world, she would show them to her friends at school and at night she would look at them and cry, she would keep them in a little box . . .

Which way should he go? People would assume he had headed towards Saint-Hilaire, so he should set off in the opposite direction, he did not know where it led because when you drove out of Beauval, it was always through Saint-Hilaire. He would look it up on a map.

His mind was racing. Instantly coming up with a solution to every problem. Marmont train station was eight kilometres away, he would walk there after dark, keeping well away from the main road. Once he arrived, he would need to buy a ticket, but to make sure he was not recognised, he would ask someone else to buy it for him, he was pleased with this plan. He would pick a woman, that would be easier. He would say that his mother had dropped him off at the station and forgot to give him his ticket before she drove off, he would show the woman his money . . . Money! How much did he have in his savings account?

He raced downstairs, yanked the drawer of the console table in the hall so hard it almost toppled over, the savings book was there! His father had been scrupulously putting money into it every birthday. 1,565 francs! Until this moment, the figure had been an abstract notion, his mother had always said it was his to spend, but "not until you're eighteen, and only on something useful". She had made an exception just once, last year (and even then after fierce resistance), so he could buy the diver's watch.

The watch . . .

Antoine shook himself.

More than 1,500 francs in his savings account. He could go a long way with that, hold out for a hell of a long time.

He took the savings book back up to his room, more excited than ever. Now, he need to sort things out, to be methodical. He was eager to choose his destination. First off, a train to Paris? Or maybe Marseille? Australia and South America seemed to him the safest destinations, but he wondered whether it was possible to get there from Marseille . . . He would find out when he got there. It would be better to take a boat, he could offer to work to pay his fare and therefore keep his money until he disembarked. He glanced at the globe . . . No, he would look later . . . Tonight . . .

A suitcase – no, a rucksack, the brown one his mother kept in the basement. He dashed downstairs. Only when he got it back to the bedroom did he notice how big it was – when he put it on, it almost dragged along the ground. He wondered what he would look like at the train station with such a huge bag. Maybe it would be safer to take something smaller, his school backpack for example? He laid them next to each other on the bed. One was too big, the other too small . . . He had to decide, fast. He opted for his backpack and immediately began to stuff it with socks and T-shirts. He slipped Spiderman into the side pocket, then went downstairs and put the backpack where it usually sat and went to fetch his savings book, his passport, the letter his mother had drawn up so he could visit his father in Germany, he could never remember what it was called, oh, yes, Travel Authorisation for a Minor. Would it still be valid?

He was dithering about this when he heard the door open downstairs.

He could make out his mother's voice, but also those of Claudine and Madame Kernevel.

He crept out onto the landing.

Madame Courtin made tea while the three women carried

on the conversation they had begun in the street.

"Where on earth can the little tearaway have gone?"

"Up to the pond," Claudine was saying. "Where else could he have got himself lost? He'll have fallen in, likely as not . . ."

"Oh, I hardly think it will come to that, Claudine, dear," said Madame Kernevel, "not now the driver has been spotted again . . ."

"Wh . . . which driver?"

"Oh, really, Claudine! The one that killed the Desmedts' dog!"

Madame Kernevel's exasperation was audible. In her defence, Claudine was a sweet girl, but terribly stupid, to get anything through that thick skull of hers . . . Madame Courtin interrupted, in the pedantic tone she used when giving lectures to Antoine:

"The driver who ran over the Desmedt's dog yesterday – he was spotted this morning, his car was parked up near the pond. So he's clearly been prowling around the area . . ."

"I thought the boy just wandered off and got lost . . ."

Claudine was devastated by this new information.

"Think about it, Claudine: he hasn't been seen since one o'clock this afternoon, it's nearly six o'clock. The whole area has been searched, and I mean he can't have gone far, he's six years old!"

"So someone . . . So he's been kidnapped? Oh, God! But why?"

This time, no-one answered.

Though he could not have explained it, Antoine found it

reassuring that they thought it might be a kidnapping. He knew that this theory would deflect suspicion from him.

Behind him, he heard cars approaching. He ran back to the window.

There were three of them. Now that it was dark, the searches had been called off. A fourth car appeared. Then the mayor's official car, with the mayor himself at the wheel, pulled up and parked in the street. The men loitered on the pavement, conferring in hushed tones. Their drive and determination had sputtered out, now they seemed self-conscious, almost guilty.

Madame Desmedt did not wait for one of them to summon the courage to go and bring her the news that there was no news, she rushed out of her house, dishevelled and distraught, and listened to their accounts one after another. With each scrap of information she seemed to shrink a little more. The men straggling home empty-handed, the black night, the passing hours . . . Eventually, Monsieur Desmedt himself arrived. Shoulders sagging, he stepped out of his car. When she saw him, Bernadette staggered, Weiser just had time to catch her before she fell.

Monsieur Desmedt ran over, took his wife in his arms and this mournful cortege headed towards the house.

Bernadette's chalk-white pallor, the bags under her eyes, her visible anguish, the way she had collapsed; these things had shaken Antoine.

He wished he could give Rémi back to her.

Slowly, soundlessly, he began to sob, feeling a boundless,

harrowing grief since he knew that Bernadette would never again see her little boy alive.

Soon, she would see him dead.

Lying on a stainless-steel autopsy table, covered with a sheet. She would cling to her husband and he would put his arm around her shoulders. The morgue attendant would gently lift the sheet. She would see blue-tinged, expressionless Rémi's face, see the huge bruise that covered the right side of his head. She would break down in tears, Monsieur Desmedt would comfort her. As they left, he would nod to the *gendarme* standing guard, yes, that's him, that's our little Rémi . . .

A few minutes later, the police van showed up.

Antoine saw the *capitaine* and two of his officers walk through the garden and ring the doorbell. Then they walked back to the van, but this time accompanied by Monsieur Desmedt, who strode quickly, visibly bristling with rage. The four headed towards the van where a crowd of factory workers quickly gathered.

Hearing raised voices, Antoine opened the window.

"Where are you taking him?"

"You've no right . . ."

"Let them through," the mayor roared in a vain attempt to stop the crowd turning on the *gendarmes*.

"So the mayor is siding with the police, now? Against his own people?"

Patient and determined, the *gendarmes* forged a path through the crowd, bundled Monsieur Desmedt into the back of the van and immediately drove off.

Most of the men climbed into their cars and set off after the police van . . .

Antoine did not know what to think.

Why had they taken Rémi's father? Did they suspect him of something?

Oh, if only the police would arrest someone other than him, especially Monsieur Desmedt, who terrified him . . . He thought about Bernadette, who had just seen her husband carted off by the police. Overwhelmed by conflicting scenarios, Antoine no longer knew what to think.

Claudine and Madame Kernevel had left. Madame Courtin set about heating up their dinner.

Antoine silently returned to his preparations. His backpack was small, it was not big enough to hold everything he wanted to take, but it didn't matter, with the money he had, he could buy whatever he needed.

At about 7.30 p.m., his mother called him down to dinner.

"What a kerfuffle! Can you believe it?"

She was talking to herself as much as to Antoine.

She was still thinking of the incident as a minor news item, one of those stories that neighbours still mention years later, because she was convinced that little Rémi would reappear, because her mind could not accept the notion that that he really had disappeared. She could remember various instances of children going missing . . . As she laid the table, she chattered to Antoine.

"There was that lad, the son of a neighbour of your aunt . . . Four years old, he was. Fell asleep in the linen basket, I tell you!

Hours, they spent searching for him, they even called the police, it was the sister-in-law that found him . . ."

Just at that moment, the lights of a police car strobed the windows. Madame Courtin was the first to her feet. She opened the door.

The police van pulled to a halt, not outside the Desmedts' house, but outside their house.

Madame Courtin quickly took off her apron. Antoine stood behind her.

The young *gendarme* was walking towards them.

Antoine thought he would die.

"Sorry to trouble you, Madame Courtin, but if we could have a word with your son . . ."

As he said this, he bent down and tried to catch Antoine's eye. Madame Courtin frowned.

"Why . . . ?"

"Don't worry, it's just a formality. Antoine?"

This time, the *gendarme* did not crouch down to be on the same level as the boy.

"Can you come with me, please?

Antoine followed him into the neighbours' garden where two other officers were standing. Monsieur Desmedt was also there, his expression inscrutable. He glowered at Antoine.

The *gendarme* turned to Antoine.

"Can you point out to me the exact spot where you last saw Rémi?"

Everyone was staring at him. His mother was standing directly behind him.

What had he told Bernadette? What had he told the *gendarme*? He could not remember exactly, he was terrified of making a mistake. He had mentioned the dog, Antoine did not move, the *gendarme* repeated his question:

"Antoine, can you please point out to me the exact spot where you last saw Rémi?"

It was then that Antoine realised that the officer had deliberately taken up this position to block his view of the rubbish sacks. Everything suddenly seemed much simpler. He took a step forwards and extended his arm.

"There."

"Go and stand exactly where he was standing."

Antoine walked over to the sacks. He could picture the scene, could imagine himself walking past and seeing Rémi standing near the sacks, crying . . .

He took a few paces forwards. Here.

The *gendarme* came over to him, grabbed the first sack, dragged it towards him, opened it and glanced inside. Monsieur Desmedt looked on, his arms folded.

Bernadette was standing in the porch, a silhouette framed against the light. She was tugging the collar of her coat tightly at her throat.

"And what was Rémi doing . . . ?" the officer asked.

It was all too much. If it had only been for a few minutes, Antoine would have been able to hold up, but being here in this garden lit only by the porch light and the dim glow of the streetlamps, feeling the watchful eyes of Bernadette, of Monsieur Desmedt, of the *gendarme*, of his mother who was wondering what all this was about . . . By the people who were now gathering in the street to watch the scene.

He burst into tears.

"It's alright, lad," the *gendarme* said, putting a hand on his shoulder.

At that moment, there came a muffled beating, like the fluttering wings of some enormous far-off bird. Above the woods near Saint-Eustache, a helicopter hovered, its flickering searchlight raking the ground.

Antoine's heart beat in frantic time with the unseen blades of the helicopter as it traced circles in the night sky.

The *gendarme* turned towards Monsieur Desmedt, touched his index finger to the brim of his kepi.

"Thank you for your cooperation, sir . . . An all-points bulletin has been issued, if there is any news, we'll let you know, of course."

With his fellow officers, he headed back to the police van and drove off.

Everyone went home.

"He was trying to work out how it happened . . ." Madame Courtin said.

She closed the door, locked it and went into the living room.

Antoine stood motionless in the doorway, staring at the television screen as Rémi's face stared back, smiling, his unruly tuft of hair carefully combed into place. It was a school photograph from last year, Antoine recognised the yellow T-shirt printed with a picture of a blue elephant.

The newsreader was giving a description of the boy: what he had been wearing when he disappeared, the theories as to the route he might have taken. His height was given as one metre fifteen. Who knows why, but this figure broke Antoine's heart.

There was a call for witnesses, a telephone number scrolled past at the bottom of the screen. There was talk of sending divers up to drag the pond. Antoine imagined the emergency services, lights whirling, vans parked on the path leading up to the pond, frogmen sitting on the edges of inflatable dinghies, tipping backwards into the water in one quick, expert movement . . .

The newsreader was a woman of about forty. Antoine had often seen her on television, but today he saw her differently because she was talking about them, in a grave, solemn tone: "Initial searches have proved fruitless . . ."

There was footage of Beauval that seemed somewhat dated, archive footage no doubt. A few scenes of the police cars that were supposedly driving around the town.

". . . and with nightfall, investigators had to call off the searches until tomorrow."

Antoine could not tear his eyes from the screen. He had an overpowering feeling of *déjà vu*, here was a tragic news story of the kind he had seen so often, but this time, he was directly involved because he was the killer.

". . . judicial inquiry has been launched into the circumstances surrounding the disappearance by the public prosecutor's office in Villeneuve."

"Are you coming to eat, Antoine?" Madame Courtin said.

She turned to look at her son and saw that he was deathly pale.

"If you're coming down with something, I wouldn't be at all surprised . . ."

5

Antoine barely ate, which is to say he ate nothing. Not hungry.

"I'm not surprised," his mother said, "what with all that's been going on . . ."

Antoine helped to clear the table, then, as he did every night, he went over to her, proffered his cheek for a kiss and went up to his room.

He needed to get ready, to finish packing – what time could he leave without being seen? In the middle of the night . . .

He dragged his backpack from under the bed, then felt a nagging doubt: how was he going to get the money out of his savings account?

On the rare occasions his mother allowed him to withdraw money – as she had when he bought the diver's watch – it was she who had gone to the Post Office, you can't do it yourself, you have to be eighteen . . . He would step up to the counter, they would ask to see his *carte d'identité*, not even that, they would take one look at him and that would be enough, no, sorry, I'm afraid it's impossible, sonny, you'll have to come back with your mother or father.

With no money, he could not possibly run away.

This ruined his whole plan. There was nothing he could do but stay here and wait to be arrested.

He felt upset, of course, but less so than he would have expected. He saw the trappings of his room through new eyes and immediately everything seemed ridiculous, the backpack stuffed with socks and T-shirts, the Spiderman action figure sticking out of the side pocket.

He had been carried away by the notion of running away, of becoming a fugitive, but would he actually have done it?

He felt crippled with tiredness. He had no tears left to cry. He was simply exhausted.

He pushed his backpack under the bed, slipped his savings book and his papers into a desk drawer and lay down on the bed.

His sleep was haunted by dreams of staggering towards the huge, fallen beech tree with Rémi on his back. Again and again, he saw the child's limp, dangling arms flashing before his eyes. But he could not seem to move. However much he struggled, the distance to the tree seemed constantly to reset itself. It was just as it had been in real life, the fluorescent green strap of his watch, though it seemed much bigger, impossible to not notice. Rémi had vanished from his shoulders. In his place, Antoine was carrying this huge wristwatch that weighed more than the boy. He was tramping through the forest, moving away from Saint-Eustache. Hearing a noise somewhere behind him, he stopped and turned.

It was Rémi. Lying on his belly in the dark crevasse. He was not dead, merely injured, but he was in terrible pain, his legs and ribs were broken. He was reaching up his hand towards the edge of the pit, up towards the light. Towards Antoine. He was screaming for help, for someone to help him climb out of the pit. He did not want to die.

Antoine!

Rémi went on screaming.

Antoine wanted to help, but his feet refused to move, he could see the little boy reaching out to him, could hear his pleas rise to a terrible wail . . .

Antoine!

Antoine!

He woke with a start. His mother was sitting on the edge of his bed, looking at him worriedly. She was wringing her hands.

Antoine . . .

He sat up, instantly awake. Everything came flooding back. What time was it?

The only light in the bedroom was a faint yellow glow from downstairs.

"You gave me such a fright, screaming like that . . . Is something wrong, Antoine?"

Antoine swallowed hard. He shook his head.

"Tell me, Antoine, is something wrong?"

Was this the moment to confess everything? If he had been more awake, he would probably have given in to temptation, anything to rid himself of this weight that was too much for him to bear, he would have told his mother everything. Everything. But he could not quite work out what was happening.

"Sleeping there fully clothed, with your shoes on and every-thing . . . It's not like you . . . If you're not feeling well, why don't you just tell me?"

His mother laid a hand on his arm; he pulled away, he did not like her being physically affectionate. She was not offended, boys are like that, she had read an article about it somewhere, you shouldn't take these things personally, it was a phase, he would get over it.

"Are you feeling sick?"

"I'm fine," Antoine said.

Madame Courtin placed her hand on his forehead, the same familiar gesture she always made.

"This whole thing has upset you, that's only natural. And being questioned by the police, well, obviously, you're not used to it . . ."

She looked at him, smiling tenderly. Usually, this was some-thing Antoine found irritating, stop looking at me like that, I'm not a baby, but this time he allowed himself to be comforted. He closed his eyes.

"Go on, now," his mother said after a moment, "get undressed and get into bed."

She left the bedroom door open.

It was dawn before Antoine finally fell asleep.

6

At first light the helicopter from the *sécurité civile* began circling again. It droned past at regular intervals, people looked up, watched as it flew over. *Gendarmes* from other towns in the *département* arrived to provide reinforcements for the officers in Beauval. Vans and police cars criss-crossed the town centre, heading out to scour the country roads.

Soon, Rémi would have been missing for twenty-four hours.

In the shops, where snippets of news were exchanged, there was a deep pessimism. And a nebulous anger directed some-times at the *gendarmerie* and sometimes at the mayor's office. After all, the *gendarme*s had taken their time before starting an investigation into the disappearance, hadn't they? By rights, they should have started searching straight away. On the extent of the delay, opinions were varied, some claimed three hours (three hours is a long time when a six-year-old is missing!), others insisted it was more than five; in fact, their calculations differed because they were starting from different points. People had realised the little boy was missing around noon, hadn't they? Not at all – it was at about two o'clock when Madame Desmedt had begun to worry and asked around the shops. That doesn't make sense, Rémi walked part of the way to work with his father, and his afternoon shift at the factory doesn't start until a quarter to two. Alright, Madame Kernevel said, we can't be sure of the precise time, but even so, it was up to the mayor's office to do something. On this point, almost everyone was agreed, after all Monsieur Weiser had not even wanted to get the *gendarmes* involved! He kept saying the kid would come back and we'd all look stupid for having called them in for no reason!

Antoine did not leave his bedroom, He tried to concentrate on playing with his Transformers and kept an eye on the Desmedts' garden where nothing much appeared to be happening. Monsieur Desmedt had left at dawn to search for Rémi and had not been seen since.

Antoine's mother was constantly coming and going with snippets of information that contradicted what she had told him previously.

In the late morning, a van from a local television station drove into town, a female journalist interviewed passers-by; the crew came and shot footage of the Desmedts' house, then left.

Madame Courtin came home towards noon and announced that one of the teachers at the local secondary school had been helping the police with their enquiries since early morning, but she could not put a name to him.

Shortly afterwards, an update began to circulate: the frogmen from the *sécurité civile* would begin dragging the pond at

2.00 p.m. Madame Courtin went round to Bernadette to try to convince her not to go (and she was not the only one), but she was wasting her breath. By 1.30 p.m., a dozen people had gathered in the garden to insist they would go with her, some offering to help, others to support her. They set off as though they were going to a funeral, they did not look as though they held out much hope.

Antoine watched them leave. Should he go too? In the end he decided he would go only because he knew they would find nothing.

The street was thronged with people. From a distance, it would have been difficult to tell whether it was a procession or a day trip.

Sitting in a wicker chair out on the pavement, Madame Antonetti watched the populace of Beauval troop past with a brazen contempt they had long since learned to ignore.

The *gendarmes* had erected safety barriers to prevent people from getting too close to the pond, the divers had to be left to work in peace. When Bernadette arrived, flanked by Claudine and Madame Courtin, the duty officer did not know what to do. You can hardly prevent the boy's mother from being present, people muttered indignantly. The officer hesitated, but the safety barriers were already beginning to shake, there were catcalls, someone shouted an insult, the feverish atmosphere that had marked the investigation from the start bubbled up again. In the end, the officer thought it best to stand aside, only to have to ask: who should he allow past the barrier to support Bernadette?

Fortunately, the *capitaine de gendarmes* arrived. Without a second thought, he took Bernadette by the arm and personally led her to the police van where he offered her tea from his thermos. From this position, she could see nothing of what was happening on the pond, but at least she was there.

Antoine kept his distance. Émilie came to join him. She was about to strike up a conversation, but she did not have time before first Théo and Kevin, and then all the other boys and girls showed up. They had adopted the manner and the words of their parents. Some of them knew Rémi only vaguely, but already it felt as though he was their little brother, just as he had become every parent's son.

"It was Monsieur Guénot who got arrested by the police," Théo said.

This revelation caused a ripple of shock. Monsieur Guénot was a science teacher, a fat guy who had attracted various rumours. People claimed to have seen him coming out of certain establishments in Saint-Hilaire . . .

Émilie turned to Théo in surprise.

"Monsieur Guénot's not under arrest, we saw him this morning!"

Théo was categorical:

"If you saw him this morning, you saw him before he was arrested. But I can guarantee that he's being held by the police now and that . . . you know, I probably shouldn't tell you any more."

It was infuriating, this way he had of withholding information just to make people beg, but he had always been like this, wanting to seem important. Several voices insisted they needed to know. Théo stared at his shoes, tight-lipped, as though uncertain which attitude to adopt.

"O.K. . . ." he said at last, "but you have to keep it to yourselves."

There were whispered promises. Théo lowered his voice until he was barely audible, they had to lean in to hear.

"Guénot . . . he's a queer. People are saying he's done things to pupils before . . . There were complaints, but it was all hushed up. By the headmaster, obviously. Apparently he likes them young, if you know what I mean. He's been seen hanging around the Desmedts' house a couple of times. Some people are wondering whether the headmaster isn't . . ."

The little group was stunned by this news.

Antoine, on the other hand, could not work out what was happening. Last night, the police were apparently investigating Monsieur Desmedt, but then they just dropped it. This morning, it was Monsieur Guénot. And maybe even the headmaster. The police had moved the search to the pond, where Antoine knew they would find nothing. For the first time in twenty-four hours, he felt his chest relax a little. Was he out of danger? He could not run away, but neither could he put a lingering question out of his mind: what if Rémi was never found?

For one whole day, this patch of ground by the pond, from where no-one could see anything and no-one could go anywhere – was like an annex of Beauval; scraps of news arrived by some path no-one could retrace only to leave so heavily embellished with comments and opinions that they became major bulletins.

In mid-afternoon, a distinct connection was made between the search of the pond by the frogmen and the arrest of a man about whose identity – despite Théo's protestations – opinions were divided. In this race to be found guilty, Monsieur Guénot was on the inside track, but the road hog who had knocked down Monsieur Desmedt's dog the day before was putting up a good show. Killed stone dead, people said. Poor Roger, all he could do was put the dog into a rubbish sack, and did the guy even stop to say sorry? Did he hell! And, come to think of it, someone saw him later, spotted his car just outside Beauval, a Fiat. Or maybe a Citroën. Metallic-blue. With a Rhône number plate, they're all road hogs there. But did that happen the same day? Surely the dog was killed the day before the kid went missing? But that's what I'm saying, the Fiat came back.

Some had ventured to add two or three other names to the list of candidates, among them that of Monsieur Danesi, who ran the Scierie du Pont sawmill, but the accusation gained little credence since the source of the information was Roland, an employee Danesi had quarrelled with some weeks previously over some unresolved incident involving a theft. A rumour is a delicate sauce, either it takes or it doesn't. This one did not take.

As for Monsieur Desmedt, he was considered an outsider with little credibility. Surly, often brutish and always spoiling for a fight, he was not well-liked, nonetheless he had the undeniable advantage of being from Beauval and therefore a less likely suspect than Monsieur Guénot, who was from Lyon, to say nothing of the hit-and-run driver who might be from anywhere. No-one seriously believed that Monsieur Desmedt could have abducted and murdered his son, why would he do such a thing? Besides, the *gendarmes* had searched the route to the factory he had taken with Rémi and found nothing. In fact, even those who disliked Roger Desmedt found it difficult to believe he was guilty.

At the very thought that someone might have killed Rémi – that sweet little boy with his chubby face and his bright, twinkling eyes – conversations would trail off into a queasy silence at this image whose true horror no-one could begin to imagine. Even Antoine could not picture it, because as the afternoon dragged on, his experience of the event had been transformed. He had been the second-last person to see Rémi alive. This fact alone provoked heated discussions. Had Antoine seen Rémi before or after the boy had walked part of the way to work with his father? This was a serious question. It was a matter of minutes and was impossible to determine. And so Antoine was forced to recount the scene over and over. People would gather round him and for the umpteenth time they would listen to him explain how he came out of his house, they would picture little Rémi hunkered by the shed his father had demolished, imagine the rubbish sacks, one of which contained the body of the dog. Antoine himself eventually came to believe this fiction; each time he told it, he could see it, he was there; in his mind and that of those who listened, the story took on the weight and heft of truth.

Théo Weiser, having lost his starring role, stayed in the background. Antoine watched out of the corner of his eye. Théo, constantly surrounded by school friends, would whisper and give him sidelong glances . . .

Though Antoine did not know why, he and Théo had never hit it off. He, Émilie and Théo formed a strange, unofficial triangle: Antoine was a bright pupil, he had just graduated from his first term in *sixième* with excellent marks in almost every subject. Émilie was the sort of average student who, when they reach *troisième*, is channelled into whatever subjects are fashionable that year. Théo was bottom of his class, but clever enough that he had only once been forced to repeat a year. He was a year older than Antoine and Émilie, and they were not in the same class, he was with Kevin and Paul.

The fact that they were the only two pupils from Beauval in their class, that they had known each other all their lives and saw each other every day, should have brought Antoine and Émilie closer, but try as he might . . . His last attempt to ask her out up at the tree house had ended in dismal failure. Antoine did not really know how to talk to girls. With Émilie, it was even worse. And yet, before this incident, she had been in all his dreams, all his fantasies . . .

The divers stopped their work at about 5.00 p.m. and the few remaining onlookers began to head back to Beauval.

Antoine quickened his step so he could walk with Émilie, who was ahead with a gaggle of girls. He soon noticed that he was not exactly welcome. No-one would look him in the eye, no-one spoke to him. Had he gone too far in telling his story so many times? Did they resent him for attracting so much attention? Unable to bear it any longer, he grabbed Émilie by the arm and took her to one side.

"It's Théo," she said eventually.

This did not come as a surprise.

"He's just jealous."

"No, no," said Émilie. "It's not that . . ."

She looked away, but actually she was dying to tell Antoine everything, so he did not have to press her very hard.

"He's saying that you were the last person to see Rémi and . . ."

"And what?"

Émilie's tone became grave and anxious:

"And that Rémi often followed you into the woods . . ."

A shudder ran through Antoine's body, he felt suddenly cold, as though frozen stiff.

"He says that instead of dragging the pond, they'd be better off searching up by Saint-Eustache . . ."

This was a disaster.

Émilie stared at him for a long while, head tilted slightly, trying to unravel the truth from the lies. Antoine stood, unable to move, shocked by this revelation. Théo truly was a spiteful, vindictive bastard, he was a bully; it did not occur to Antoine that, unwittingly, Théo had hit upon the truth.

It was Émilie's questioning look that prompted him to act.

Without giving a thought to the situation or the possible consequences, he set off at a run towards the group ahead. As he ran, he stretched out both arms and hit Théo in the back, shoving him hard and sending him sprawling. The girls started screaming. Antoine leaped on Théo, straddled his chest and began pounding his face with both fists. It made a sound that none of them had ever heard, muffled, visceral . . . Théo was bigger and stronger than Antoine, but the attack had caught him off guard. By the time he managed to throw off his attacker, his face was streaming blood. Antoine landed heavily on his side, he saw Théo struggling to get up, but he was faster. In an instant he was on his feet, frantically looking around for a stone. He bent to grab a large branch and, as Théo staggered towards him, he raised it in both hands and brought it crashing down on his face.

The branch was about forty centimetres long and quite thick, but it was completely rotted through.

It broke against Théo's skull with a spongy sound. Antoine found himself holding a length of jagged wood the colour of a mushroom.

The little group was so shocked by the incident that no-one noticed how preposterous it was. Though it had ended in a pathetic farce, Antoine had just launched an attack on an authority that had never before been challenged.

Several adults rushed over to separate the boys. Shouting and fretting, they reached for handkerchiefs and cleaned up the blood. Thankfully it was nothing serious, only a split lip.

The crowd moved off again, trudging back to Beauval.

The teenagers spontaneously split into two groups. More of them sided with Antoine than with Théo.

Antoine nervously ran his fingers through his hair, flustered, he was unsettled by the troubling similarity . . . Twice in the past two days he had lashed out and hit a boy with a stick. The first boy, the one who did not deserve it, was dead.

Was he going to becoming one of the vicious, indiscriminate bullies he had seen so often in the school playground?

He noticed Émilie was walking beside him. Though he could not have said why, this fact did little to reassure him. This obsession girls had with thugs . . .

Shortly before 5.00 p.m., the police van drove Bernadette Desmedt home. The sight of this woman crushed by grief was heart-wrenching.

While he waited for his mother to come home, Antoine turned on the television and watched the news report about the worrying disappearance of little Rémi Desmedt. There was footage of Beauval, first came the church, then the *mairie*. Then came the main street. In a rather pathetic attempt to dramatise the situation – since the reporter on location had nothing to say – the camera panned through the town centre and out towards little Rémi's house.

Antoine felt a lump in his throat as he watched the main street flash past, the town square, the grocer's shop, the school . . .

The camera was closing in, not on Rémi's house, but on his own. It was not searching for the child, but for him.

Now the footage showed his street, the Mouchottes' house with its shutters painted British racing green, then the garden of the Desmedts' house. In order to dramatise and accentuate the void left by the little boy's disappearance, the camera slowly swung around, lingering on the abandoned swing, on the garden gate the boy would have pushed when he left . . .

The camera pulled back, the wide shot taking in a section of the Courtins' garden, and Antoine waited, expecting it to scan the façade, to gradually zoom in and end on a close-up of his face: "And this is the boy who killed Rémi Desmedt and buried his body in the woods at Saint-Eustache, where it will be discovered by the *gendarmerie* tomorrow morning."

Antoine could not help himself, he quickly retreated and ran upstairs to hide out in his bedroom.

Madame Courtin eventually came back from doing the shopping, it had taken three times longer than usual. Antoine could hear her bustling around in the kitchen before she came upstairs to his room. She looked distraught.

"It's not one of the teachers at the school they've arrested . . ."

Antoine looked up from his Transformers and stared at his mother.

"It's Monsieur Kowalski."

7

Madame Courtin and her son were both shaken by this arrest. Though he felt wretched at the idea, Antoine could not help but think that if Monsieur Kowalski were found guilty – he did not trouble to wonder how such a verdict might be possible – it would bother him less than if it were someone else. His mother had always hated working for the man, he had a terrible reputation in the town, he even *looked* evil. The fruitless searches, the pond that had been dragged to no avail, and now the arrest of Frankenstein . . . Antoine had begun to believe that the nightmare might be ending, that he might be safe, but that was to forget Théo, whose spiteful innuendos might lead the police to him. How far might Théo go? What if he told his father? What if he told the *gendarmes*?

Antoine was furious with himself for giving in to his anger, for attacking Théo, he should have left things as they were, he had been stupid.

"Monsieur Kowalski . . ." Madame Courtin muttered. "Well I never . . ."

She was clearly troubled by the news.

"What do you care?" said Antoine, "You never liked him."

"Well, no, but even so . . . It's different when you know someone personally."

She stood for a moment in silence. Antoine assumed she was considering the impact of this arrest on her life, on her work, she was obviously worried.

"You can get a job somewhere else. You were always complaining about him, you never wanted to go to work."

"Really? I suppose you think it's easy to just find another job?"

She was angry now.

"Try telling that to the factory workers Monsieur Weiser is planning to lay off in the New Year . . . !"

Rumours of forthcoming redundancies had been doing the rounds in Beauval for weeks now. Whenever he was asked about it, Monsieur Weiser was cagey. He did not know yet, it would depend on a number of factors, he would have to wait for the quarterly accounts . . . The workers had noticed that orders had increased over the past two months, but this was something that happened every year in the run-up to Christmas. Monsieur Weiser had been forced to rehire staff he had laid off three months earlier, though on a part-time basis, for a few hours a week. Even Monsieur Mouchotte had gone back to work for several weeks. But was the upturn enough to make up for a disastrous autumn, when the order books had been empty? No-one knew.

Antoine often wondered whether his mother really needed

to work. She railed against Monsieur Kowalski, all the years she'd been working for him, and for what? Antoine did not know, but it was obviously not much, were they really so poor? Madame Courtin had never complained about the maintenance her ex-husband paid. "I can't fault him on that score, at least . . ." she would sometimes say, leaving Antoine to wonder on what other scores she could fault him.

"Right, well, we can't just sit around here," she said finally, "You need to get yourself ready."

She was preoccupied by something else.

Christmas Mass, which rotated among the surrounding towns each year, was to take place in Beauval. This year, Midnight Mass was scheduled for 7.30 p.m., since the parish priest had to criss-cross the *département* to give six Masses one after another.

Madame Courtin's relationship with religion was sensible and pragmatic. She had sent Antoine to Sunday School as a precaution, but when he did not want to go anymore, she had not insisted. She went to church when she needed help. God was a distant neighbour it was pleasant to bump into occasionally, someone you felt you could ask a small favour of from time to time. She went to Mass at Christmas in the way some people might visit an elderly aunt. Her utilitarian approach to religion was largely a matter of conformism.

Madame Courtin had been born here, she had been raised and still lived in a small town where everybody knew everybody else's business, where what the neighbours thought was a crushing weight. In everything, Madame Courtin did what *ought* to be done, simply because it was what everyone around her did. She cared about her reputation the same way she cared about her home and probably as much as she cared about life itself, since she was the sort of person who was quite capable of dying from a lack of respectability. To Antoine, Midnight Mass was just one more of the duties he had to submit to each year so that his mother – at least in her own eyes – could continue to seem like a fine, upstanding woman.

As everywhere else, the faithful in Beauval were not as numerous as they had once been. If the Sunday Masses throughout the year managed to attract a sizeable congregation it was thanks to those who flocked from Marmont, Montjoue, from Fuzelières, from Varennes as well as those from Beauval itself.

On the whole, religious worship was a seasonal affair. Most of the faithful came to church only when the harvest was poor, when the price of livestock plummeted or when local factories were planning lay-offs. The church offered a service, and the congregation behaved like consumers. Even important cyclical events like Christmas, Easter or the Assumption were a factor in this utilitarian approach. They were a means for the customers to pay their subscription so that, during the year, they could make use of the service as necessary. As a result, Midnight Mass at Christmas was always a roaring success.

Shortly after 7.00 p.m., the residents of Beauval began to assemble at the town square. They should have been pleased to see the church so thronged, but any pleasure was spoiled by the fact that many of the congregation were not from Beauval.

The women went into the church as soon as they arrived, while the men loitered for a few minutes in the churchyard, smoking a cigarette, shaking hands, making small talk, bumping into clients they had not seen in an age, women they used to sleep with, even a few old friends from whom, over time, they had become a little estranged.

The disappearance of Rémi Desmedt had stoked a certain curiosity which went some way to explaining the swelling crowds. They had all seen Beauval on the nightly news bulletin, and in coming here, those who did not live in the town were attempting to square two very different images: the familiar humdrum town where nothing ever happened, and the news of this terrible incident that, with each passing hour, loomed more like a tragedy.

Thirty hours had elapsed, and the disappearance of little Rémi was now considered deeply disturbing.

Everyone was speculating about what would happen.

When would he be found? And what exactly would they find?

On the steps of the church, this was all anyone could talk about as conversations gradually drifted towards the arrest of Monsieur Kowalski. Madame Mouchotte was listening, wide-eyed, to Claudine who had just happened to be in Kowalski's shop when the *gendarmes* arrived.

"It was all over in the space of five minutes, and that's God's honest truth. And Kowalski didn't look too cocky, let me tell you . . ."

Madame Courtin said:

"But . . . what exactly is he being accused of?"

Something about an alibi. Someone had heard someone else say that Kowalski's van had been spotted parked on the edge of the woods on the outskirts of Beauval.

"So where exactly was that filthy animal when it happened?" asked another in the group.

"It's not exactly what you might call proof!" said Madame Courtin. "Not that I'm making excuses for him, obviously not, but even so . . . If a man can't even drive his car without being accused of abducting a child, well, I don't know . . ."

"That's not the point!" said Madame Antonetti.

She spoke in a strident tone, enunciating every syllable as though it were her last, which gave a clipped, peremptory tone to her pronouncements that many found persuasive. Everyone immediately turned to her.

"The simple fact is that this man Kowalski (I've never set foot in that shop of his, perish the thought!), he can't account for his whereabouts during the period when the child disappeared! His van was sighted, but Kowalski claims he can't remember what he was doing . . ."

She said this with such conviction that no-one would have thought to ask where she had come by this information. Especially as she was the primary and usually the best source of gossip in Beauval, and was therefore entitled to conclude ominously:

"You have to admit it's all very peculiar, no?"

Madame Courtin nodded, yes, it is peculiar, it seems almost suspicious . . . But she did not seem entirely convinced.

Antoine left his mother and ran to catch up with a pack of school friends in their Sunday best who had been forced to come to Mass too. Émilie was wearing a flower-print dress that looked as though it had been cut from a curtain roll, she seemed somehow more frizzy-haired, more blonde, more animated than usual, as pretty as a princess, a fact confirmed by the calculated indifference of all the boys present. Her parents, the most faithful of the faithful, never missed Mass, they had sent Émilie to Sunday School since she was a little girl. Madame Mouchotte was capable of going to Mass three times in one day, her husband was the only man who sang in the choir where he shamelessly drowned out everyone with a booming voice that communicated the fervour of his faith. Émilie did not believe in God, but was so devoted to her mother that she would have become a nun if she had been asked.

A great silence fell over the group as Antoine joined them. Théo, who smelled of cigarette smoke, stared pointedly at his shoes. His lip was swollen and flushed dark red with a small scab. He could not help but shoot Antoine a black look. But he was shrewd enough to know that everyone was more interested in the sudden arrest of Frankenstein than in his squabbles with Antoine. In fact, he was promptly confronted by Kevin:

"You see? It wasn't Monsieur Guénot who was arrested at all! That was just bullshit."

Among his many other faults, Théo was never wrong. In this, he was like his father, it was a trademark of the Weiser family, they never backed down. In such circumstances, it was more crucial than ever for him to regain the upper hand.

"No, it wasn't!" Théo snapped back. "They arrested Guénot and released him, but they're still keeping an eye on him, you can take my word for it. He's definitely queer, that's for sure. And he's weird . . ."

"But still!" Kevin said, happy to have the mayor's son over a barrel for once.

"But still? But still what?" Théo was angry now.

"But still, Frankenstein's the one that they arrested."

A murmur of approval rippled through the group. The arrest neatly reinforced the popular opinion, magnificently summed up by Kevin in a single phrase:

"You only have to look at him . . ."

Though he had lost the upper hand, Théo was not about to give up the battle, and attempted an audacious flanking manoeuvre:

"I know a damn sight more than the lot of you about the case! That kid . . . he's dead!"

Dead . . .

The word set the room spinning.

"What d'you mean, he's dead?"

The conversation suddenly trailed off. Maître Vallenères had just arrived, and the sight of the lawyer pushing his daughter in her wheelchair made everyone fall silent. She was fifteen and so painfully thin that her fists would easily have passed through a napkin ring. Her only hobby was decorating her wheelchair. No-one had ever seen her do it, but there were rumours that she had ordered a special mask so she could spray-paint it. The chair was a constantly changing wonder, she had recently had two car radio antennas fitted that made it look like a giant, multicoloured insect. Some kids called her Mad Max. The joyful brilliance of her creation contrasted sharply with her face, always engrossed, uninterested in the world, people said that she was fiercely intelligent, but she would die young, and it is true that it was difficult not to imagine her being swept away by a gust of wind some day. There were many children her age in Beauval, but she did not spend time with any of them. Or perhaps none of them spent time with her. She was home-schooled, and was taught by a live-in tutor she had had since she first fell ill.

The sight of the outlandish wheelchair rolling into the church was like a provocation. People wondered whether God might not punish her lack of propriety. She and her father were followed by Madame Antonetti, the spiteful bitch who never missed an opportunity to observe these people she had scorned and despised with every fibre of her being since the dawn of time.

"Are they sure he's dead?" Kevin said in a harsh whisper as soon as they had passed.

It was a stupid question, given that the body had not been found, but it perfectly communicated the confusion the little group felt at the very idea of murder. The very word was enough to take your breath away. Antoine wondered whether Théo had said this so he could be the centre of attention, or whether he actually knew something.

"And anyway, how would you know?" Kevin said.

"My father . . ." Théo said, and allowed the word hang in

the air, then he looked down at the ground and solemnly shook his head with the air of one who knows but cannot say. Antoine could not bear it any longer.

"What about your father?"

Since the fight that afternoon, a comment by Antoine carried considerably more weight. It forced Théo to embellish. He glanced over his shoulder to make sure he was not overheard.

"He had a word with the *capitaine* at the *gendarmerie* . . . They know what happened."

"What do they know?"

"Let's just say . . ." Théo took a long, deep breath. "They've found evidence. They know where to look for the body. It's only a matter of hours . . . I can't really say any more . . ."

He looked at Antoine, at Émilie, then at the others and mumbled: ". . . Sorry."

Then he slowly turned on his heel, crossed the square and went into the church.

It was obviously a bluff, but why had Théo looked at Antoine first? Émilie took a lock of hair between her thumb and forefinger and twisted it thoughtfully. If she was going out with Théo (Antoine did not know one way or the other), was she in on the secret? She had not participated in the discussion, had not said a word . . . Antoine could not bring himself to look at her.

"Right, I'm off," she said.

She peeled away from the group and went into the church.

Antoine had an overwhelming urge to run away. And he

would probably have done just that if, at that moment, his mother had not appeared.

"Come on, Antoine!"

All around, men were stubbing out cigarettes, doffing their hats and their caps, then the church doors slowly swung shut.

What child is this, who laid to rest, on Mary's lap is sleeping? Whom angels greet with anthems sweet, While shepherds watch are keeping?

Next to his mother, Antoine was sitting at the edge of the pew immediately beside the central aisle; right in front of him was the nape of Émilie's neck, something that usually had profound effect on him, but not tonight. Théo's words rattled around in his head. They had evidence . . . Unconsciously, he felt his wrist. If it was true, then what were they waiting for? Why had they not come for him straight away?

Maybe during the Mass . . .

Welcome to you all on this Christmas night where we joyfully celebrate the birth of the Christ child.

The priest was a young, fat, clean-shaven man with thick lips and piercing eyes. He moved at a slight angle, as though he was shy, as though afraid to trouble anyone, but spurred by a fervent, harsh, demanding faith that starkly contrasted with his physique. It was not difficult to picture him, naked, pudgy, pot-bellied, furiously flagellating himself in a monastic cell.

. . . He who summons us, who fills us with all Joy and Peace in believing, that we may abound in hope . . .

To the left of the altar, a small group of women were gathered around Madame Mouchotte, who stood head and shoulders above them, and in front of them, the little church organ that Madame Kernevel had played for more than thirty years.

At regular intervals, heads furtively glanced back at the church doors. People were disappointed that the Desmedts had not made an appearance. It was perfectly understandable, but all the same, Christmas Mass . . . Heads turned towards the door, people whispered.

Then, finally, they arrived.

They walked arm in arm, like an old married couple. Bernadette looked as though she had shrunk by several more centimetres. Her face was chalk-white, there were deep circles under her eyes. Monsieur Desmedt was tight-lipped, a man struggling to contain himself. They were followed by Valentine, their daughter, wearing a pair of red trousers that seemed shameful in the church, in the circumstances. Summing up general opinion, Émilie said she was "the town bicycle", a phrase that Antoine found both shocking and oddly intriguing.

As they passed, Antoine got a whiff of Monsieur Desmedt's harsh, acrid smell.

As they continued on their way, Antoine watched Valentine's pert red buttocks jiggle with an extraordinary expressivity that left a strange taste in his mouth like someone else's saliva.

Lord Jesus, sent by the Father for the salvation of the world.

The Desmedt family slowly made their way up the long central aisle.

Although the Mass did not stop for them, in their wake

there settled a very different silence, murmurous, reverential, solicitous, sorrowful and sombre.

Father, you make this holy night radiant with the splendour of the true light; grant in your grace that, enlightened by the revelation of this mystery, we might one day enter into eternal joy in the kingdom of heaven. Through Jesus Christ, your Son, our Lord.

The entrance of the Desmedts had been like the arrival of the penitents. Bernadette had found it a struggle to walk. Monsieur Desmedt moved through the transept slowly but with animal determination, head bowed, tread heavy, it seemed as though he was intending to have things out with the priest, to do battle with God Himself.

When they came to the altar, they stopped. There was no room in the front pew. They turned as though about to head back down the nave and leave the church. Valentine was now standing next to her mother, all three of them facing the flock of parishioners. And there was something heart-wrenching about the tableau: this bull-necked man straining to keep his rage in check, this ravaged woman and their adolescent daughter who oozed sex and disappointment. It was as though the family, from whom little Rémi was conspicuously absent, were offering up their suffering to God.

No-one knew what would happen next. Though he was sitting some distance away, Antoine felt the savage energy that emanated from Monsieur Desmedt when, finally, he raised his head and stared at the assembled townspeople. He shot a quick glance at Monsieur Mouchotte, who had cordially loathed Rémi's father ever since the altercation at the factory when Monsieur Desmedt had slapped him. It is true that Monsieur Desmedt's frequent outbursts had made him many enemies. Faced with this harrowing spectacle, the people in the front pew suddenly began to stir, several people quickly got to their feet in order to free up some space and crept down the side aisle to stand at the back of the church. The Desmedt family sat down. Facing the priest who was officiating.

For unto us a child is born, unto us a Son is given . . .

As soon as the Desmedts had disappeared from his view, Émilie turned to Antoine and stared at him with a curious insistence.

Was her look a question? What did she know?

He frantically tried to interpret the meaning of her look, but she had already turned away. Had this been a message? What was she trying to tell him?

She had been strangely silent when Théo had said, "They know where to look for the body". Instinctively, he glanced towards the door of the church.

"They've found evidence . . ."

Then it burst over him like an explosion, Antoine suddenly knew that with her look Émilie was telling him not to stay here.

To run. That was it. They were waiting for Mass to be over in order to arrest him. He had walked right into their trap. Outside, there would be a police cordon . . .

Tomorrow the wickedness of the earth will be destroyed and the saviour of the world will reign over us.

Antoine would find himself trapped by the horde of the

faithful stampeding towards the doors. Gradually, they would turn back, scanning the crowd to see what could have prompted the forces of law and order to gather on the church steps in the middle of the night on Christmas Eve. Soon, Antoine would find himself alone, walking down the aisle, the crowd parting as he passed.

The screaming would start . . .

He would have no choice but to surrender to the *gendarmes* or wait as the heavy footsteps of Monsieur Desmedt drew level with him. Antoine would turn around to find Rémi's father shouldering his rifle, the barrel pointed at Antoine's head.

Antoine let out a scream, but it was drowned out by another. Rémi!

In the front pew, Bernadette was on her feet, wailing for her son. Valentine tugged at her sleeve and slowly she took her seat again.

Startled by the cry, Madame Kernevel's fingers froze on the organ and the choir trailed off into awkward silence.

Then the voice of Monsieur Mouchotte boomed out, the organ immediately followed suit and the choir once again took up the hymn in resolute chorus, bidding the congregation to stand fast against the chaos.

On this night, when the mercy and kindness of God our Saviour have appeared, let us, dear brothers and sisters, humbly pour forth to him our prayers, trusting not in our own good works, but in his mercy.

The priest carried on with the Mass and greeted each of these mishaps – the appearance of the Desmedts, the erring of both organ and choir – with an infinitesimal smile that expressed his jubilation that he had been called upon by God to exemplify rigorous morality in the face of a congregation that was obviously losing its bearings. The chaotic nature of the service merely confirmed how much his flock needed to find in him a brother, a father who might show them the way. Overcome by events beyond their understanding, the faithful followed the Mass with the resignation of the damned.

Antoine had managed to calm himself: it was unthinkable that the *gendarmes* would defer the arrest of a child-killer; as soon as they had conclusive evidence, they would dispatch officers to arrest him. Théo's pronouncements had simply been a means to avoid him losing face. After all, the insinuations he had been making last night had been proved incorrect by the arrest of Frankenstein. Antoine knew that the Marmont *charcutier* had nothing to confess, he knew they would have to release him soon. What would happen then?

. . . and the angel said to the shepherds, Fear not: for, behold, I bring you good tidings of great joy, which shall be to all people. For unto you is born this day in the city of David a Saviour, which is Christ the Lord . . .

Believing he had the congregation in the palm of his hand, the young priest began his homily in a deep, solemn voice, borne up by the will of God he was charged with communicating.

Naturally, he knew what had happened in Beauval in the past few days (he was reputed to be the best-informed man in the district), he knew young Rémi, having seen the boy attend Sunday Mass with his mother (her husband was rarely seen).

On this Christmas Eve, he thought of the child as a sort of cherub. He gazed at the parents in the front pew and, all around them, at the solemn, sorrowful faces, as though somehow by a process of osmosis their grief had spread to the whole congregation. He was unsettled by what he saw: where was the joy that the birth of Jesus should have stirred in them?

It was clear that the faithful, blinded by these disturbing events, had failed to understand the meaning of what had happened. He observed a long silence.

"Life constantly puts us to the test . . ." he began at length.

His voice was suddenly firm and clear. It echoed through the church, an effect he accentuated by drawing out the final syllables.

"But remember, '*The fruit of the Spirit is love, joy, peace, patience . . .*' Patience! Be patient and you will see!"

To judge from the faces of his flock, the message had not yet got through. He would have to explain. So the young priest set about doing just that, his voice pulsing with determination; in this rustic priest, there was a missionary aching to burst out.

"Brothers and sisters in Christ, I understand your grief. I share your pain. Like you, I too am suffering."

This was clearer, from their faces he could see that these words had touched a nerve. He felt emboldened.

"But suffering is not a misfortune . . . What is suffering? It is the most magnificent gift from God, for it serves to bring us closer to Him and to his Perfection."

He had admirably modulated the word "magnificent". He warmed to his theme, abandoning the sermon he had spent hours preparing so that he could give it in every church in the diocese. Now, his faith was speaking through him. God was guiding him. Never before had he felt himself entrusted with a greater mission.

"It's true! Because suffering, pain and grief, these are our penitence ..."

He marked a pause, propped his elbows on the pulpit, leaned towards the congregation and in a gentle voice he said:

"And what purpose does it serve, this penitence?"

The question was followed by a long silence. No-one would have been surprised to see a hand go up, like a child's at school. The priest stood up straight, jabbed his finger towards heaven, and in a commanding voice, proclaimed:

"To prevail against the evil that is within us all! God allows us to be tested so that we may reveal to Him the power of our faith!"

He turned and whispered a few inaudible words to Madame Kernevel, who nodded vigorously.

The organ immediately struck up, followed by the resounding voice of Monsieur Mouchotte. The choir gradually joined in the thanksgiving hymn:

In all things God does right by Man,
Hallelujah, let us praise him!
In his fond grace begetting children,
Hallelujah, let us praise him!
That they shall love Him as He doth them ...

One by one, the faithful joined the chorus. It was impossible to tell whether the hymn truly provided them with healing and consolation or whether it was merely a tangible expression of their devotion, but the priest was elated, he had done what needed to be done.

After the Concluding Rite and the Dismissal, he unfolded a piece of paper as he always did for parish announcements.

"To try and find our dear little Rémi, a search of the woods has been scheduled for tomorrow morning. The *gendarmerie* is calling on all those who can to volunteer. Those taking part should meet outside the *mairie* at 9.00 a.m."

Antoine was stunned by this news.

They were going to search the woods, they were going to find Rémi. This time, there would be no escape.

The information also had an immediate effect on the parishioners, there was a murmur which the young priest silenced with a peremptory gesture.

Then he launched into the final blessing, he needed to get to Montjoue, he was already running late.

8

Outside the church, men gathered around Monsieur Desmedt, laid a hand on his shoulder and muttered platitudes. Bernadette walked off without looking at anyone. Valentine stood on the opposite pavement and people could not help but wonder what she was waiting for. Hands in her jacket pockets, she watched the crowds leave the church with studied indifference.

Antoine had a knot in his stomach, he was terrified, he had no-one he could talk to. He set off for home, weaving his way through the groups of churchgoers.

Surrounded by his habitual entourage, Théo was casually letting slip a few more indiscreet details to shock and surprise his listeners. Antoine hurried along. The enmity between him and Théo was such that you could feel it in the air itself. When Antoine was finally defeated, Théo would be king of the school, of the town, no-one would challenge his authority ever again.

Antoine felt beaten, crushed, humiliated.

At the garden gate, he turned back and, in the distance,

watched his mother, arm in arm with Bernadette, trudging slowly homeward.

The piteous sight of these two women floored him: Madame Desmedt, grieving her murdered son walking side by side with Madame Courtin, the mother of his murderer . . .

Antoine pushed open the door.

The house was filled with the smell of the roasting chicken his mother had put into the oven before she went out. At the foot of the Christmas tree, there were several presents – she always managed to put them there without his noticing. He did not turn on the light. The room was illuminated only by the flickering string of fairy lights. His heart felt heavy.

Having survived the ordeal of Midnight Mass, the prospect of spending Christmas Eve with his mother was gruelling.

There were few things that escaped Madame Courtin's mania for transforming everyday events into ritual, and every year Christmas Eve was exactly the same. Over the years, something that had been a simple, unalloyed pleasure for Antoine had gradually become a ritual and then a chore. And it felt interminable. They would watch the Christmas show on T.V., have dinner at 10.30 p.m., open presents at midnight . . . Madame Courtin had never made a distinction between Christmas Eve and New Year's Eve, she planned them according to precisely the same model, down to the presents.

Antoine went up to his room to fetch the gift he had bought his mother. This was another difficult task, finding something different for her each year. He took the small package from his wardrobe, he could no longer remember what it was. A gold label in one corner read, "Tabac Loto Cadeau – 11, rue Joseph-Merlin" – Monsieur Lemercier's shop. On the left as you entered, there was a display case containing knives, alarm clocks, tablemats, notebooks . . . But try as he might, Antoine could not recall what he had bought this year.

Hearing his mother open the garden gate, he raced downstairs and put the present with the others.

Madame Courtin was hanging up her coat.

"Oh dear, oh dear, what a terrible business . . ."

Walking home arm in arm with Bernadette had upset her. A second night with little Rémi still missing, the Mass, that priest telling people they should prepare for the worst – he hadn't put it in those words, exactly, but that was what he meant – the police arresting someone she knew, in this con-catenation of events Blanche Courtin encountered something that was beyond understanding.

She took off her hat and hung it with her coat, put on her house slippers, shaking her head.

"Honestly, I ask you . . ."

"What?"

She tied her apron around her waist.

"Kidnapping a little lad like that . . ."

"Oh, give it a rest, Maman!"

But Madame Courtin was on a roll. In order to understand, she needed to conjure images:

"I mean, can you imagine? Abducting a six-year-old boy . . . ? And I mean, *why*, for God's sake?"

A vision came to her. She bit her lip and dissolved into tears.

For the first time in years, Antoine felt the urge to be close to her, to take her in his arms, reassure her, beg her forgiveness, but the sight of his mother's ravaged face made his heart lurch, he did not dare move.

"They'll end up finding that child dead, you mark my words, but what sort of state will he be in . . ."

She dabbed at her tears with the corners of the apron. Unable to bear it, Antoine dashed from the kitchen, ran up to his room and threw himself on the bed where he, too, burst into tears.

He did not hear his mother. He simply felt her gently lay her hand on the back of his neck. He did not tell her to go away. Had the time come to confess? His face buried in his pillow, Antoine desperately wanted to confess, already he was fumbling for the words. But the moment of deliverance had not yet come.

Madame Courtin was saying:

"Poor thing, you're upset by this business too, aren't you . . . ? He was such a sweet little lad, wasn't he . . . ?"

Suddenly she was talking about Rémi in the past tense. She sat for a long time, brooding on this cruel tragedy while Antoine listened to the blood pound in his temples so loudly it made his head ache.

For the first time, their end-of-year ritual was thrown out of kilter.

Madame Courtin turned on the television but did not watch. The stuffed capon was as huge as in previous years (it had to look like the colossal American turkeys seen in cartoons, they would be eating it all week), they sat down to dinner without worrying what time it was.

Antoine could eat nothing. His mother chewed a sliver of breast meat, staring at the T.V. screen. Variety-show music filled the living room accompanied by laughter and shrieking; shiny, happy presenters brandished microphones like ice-cream cones and shouted seasonal catchphrases.

Her mind on other things, Antoine's mother cleared away his plate without a word, something that was not like her. She brought in the *bûche de Noël*, the sort of cake Antoine had always loathed, and said in what she hoped was a cheery, rousing tone:

"What do you say we tackle the presents, hmm?"

For once, his father did not fail him. The parcel contained the PlayStation he had asked for, but it gave Antoine only an abstract pleasure because he felt terribly alone. Who would he play with? He could scarcely imagine that tomorrow even existed. Would he be allowed to take it with him when he was arrested?

"Now, don't forget to call your father," Madame Courtin said as she opened her own present.

She exaggerated her anticipation, I wonder what it can be . . . Finally, Antoine remembered what he had bought: a little wooden chalet that played music when you lifted the roof.

"It's beautiful!" his mother gushed, "Where on earth did you find it? It's just lovely."

She wound up the mechanism and listened to the tinkling melody, smiling as she racked her brains. It was the sort of tune everyone has heard a thousand times without ever paying attention to the name.

"Oh, I know this one," Madame Courtin murmured as she looked for the instruction booklet.

"'*Edelweiss*' (R. Rogers). Ah, yes, maybe . . ."

She stood up and kissed Antoine, who was already setting up the PlayStation. Since it came from his father, there was bound to be something wrong with it: he had hoped for "Crash Team Racing", but had got last year's version of "Gran Turismo" instead.

Madame Courtin finished clearing the table, did the washing-up, then came back into the living room with the glass of wine she had poured herself over dinner and had left untouched. She saw Antoine holding the joystick but with a faraway look in his eyes, staring at some point above the wall. She had just opened her mouth to say something when the doorbell rang.

Antoine flinched, instantly panicked.

Who could it be at this hour of the night, and on Christmas Eve . . . ?

Even Madame Courtin, who was not anxious by nature, walked warily down the hallway. She peered through the spyhole, pressing her forehead against the door, then quickly opened it.

"Valentine . . . !"

The girl apologised.

"It's my mother, she's locked herself in the bedroom, she won't come out for anyone, and she won't answer . . . Papa was wondering if . . ."

"I'll be right there."

Madame Courtin bustled between the hallway and the kitchen, taking off her apron, getting her coat . . .

"Come in, Valentine, come in . . ."

Close up, the girl looked different to how she had when Antoine had seen her earlier that evening, that condescending pout, the disdainful look. Her vivid lipstick brought out the pallor of her face. Her eyes, circled with dark-blue eyeliner, were wet with tears. She took a step towards the living room and watched as Antoine got to his feet. She gave him a curt nod and he responded with a little wave. He stared at the girl, who now seemed indifferent, as though she were alone and no-one was watching her.

She was wearing the same clothes she had worn to Mass, red jeans and a white leatherette jacket that she now unzipped with a sigh, as though suddenly realising how warm it was in the room, to reveal a pink mohair jumper that tightly hugged her bust. Antonie wondered how they could be this shape, he had never seen breasts so perfectly round. It was even possible to see her skin through the wool. The perfume she was wearing evoked some unfamiliar flower he could not quite identify . . .

"Antoine?" said Madame Courtin, already buttoned into her coat, ". . . aren't you ready?"

"Am I coming with you?" said Antoine.

"Of course you're coming. I mean, given the circumstances . . ." She shot Valentine an embarrassed look.

Antoine could not work out why "the circumstances"

required his presence. Was she saying this simply because Valentine was here?

"Right, well, I'm off. You catch me up, Antoine, O.K.?"

The prospect of going into his neighbours' house, of finding himself face to face with Monsieur Desmedt, made his stomach heave.

The door slammed shut.

He glanced around, frantically looking for a way out.

"What is this?"

He whipped around. Valentine had not gone with Madame Courtin, she was standing in front of him. She was holding the PlayStation controller, the handles pointing towards the ceiling. She grasped one of them, as though it were the hand of a hammer, and studied it curiously. Then her small, slender hand began to stroke it, tracing it with her forefinger as though to measure the smoothness, the texture, but her eyes stared deeply into Antoine's as she did so.

"What is this?" she said again.

"It's . . . for playing," Antoine stammered.

She smiled as she looked at him, still toying with the joystick.

"Oh, for playing . . ."

Antoine nodded vaguely, then scarpered, taking the stairs three at a time, he dashed into his bedroom and took a deep breath, his heart was hammering out a terrifying rhythm. He tried to remember what he had come for. Oh, yes, his shoes. He sat on the bed. Exhaustion engulfed him again, he could not resist the temptation to lie down, to close his eyes.

He could still picture Valentine's hand, still feel her magnetic presence. He was seized by an uncertainty so intense, so painful, that it rekindled his anxiety.

He was anxious to be caught, to be arrested.

Anxious to confess. To be done with it. To be able finally to sleep, to sleep.

The terrible consequences of his confession gradually faded as he was confronted with the impossibility of carrying on like this, of living with this dread, with these images. As soon as he closed his eyes, as he had now, Rémi reappeared.

The image was always the same.

The little boy lying in the dark crevasse, his hands reaching out . . .

Antoine!

Sometimes there was only one hand, struggling desperately to find some purchase, and Rémi's voice fading, as though melting away.

Antoine!

"Are you in bed already?"

Antoine sat up with a start as though he had just received an electric shock.

Valentine was standing in the doorway, she had taken off her jacket and slung it casually over her shoulder, holding it with a crooked index finger.

She surveyed the room with an inquisitiveness that had nothing to do with curiosity, took two or three steps closer, moving with a sinuous, dancing rhythm Antoine had never seen before. The perfume he had sensed earlier now permeated the whole room.

Valentine did not look at him. She slowly wandered around the room, like a blasé, indifferent visitor to a museum.

Antoine felt very hot, he tried to compose himself. He bent down, grabbed his shoes and began to lace them up, head down, eyes fixed on the floor.

He felt Valentine move closer, enter his field of vision, though it was as restricted as possible. She stood in front of him, her legs slightly parted; he could see nothing but her white trainers, the damp cuffs of her red jeans. If he had raised his head, he would be at eye level with her waist.

He carried on with his task, but his trembling hands refused to do his bidding, he had an almost painful erection. Valentine did not move. She seemed to be waiting patiently for him to finish what he was doing. So Antoine bounded to his feet, trying to step past without touching her, but there was so little room that he lost his balance and fell back on the bed. With the agility of a fish out of water, he turned over so the girl would not see the bulge in his trousers. He got to his feet again, raced to the door . . .

Valentine had not turned around. Her jacket had fallen to the floor. He was looking at her back.

Standing confidently, facing the bed, she crossed her arms and clasped her shoulders. Antoine noticed her nails were painted candy-pink. He could not stop himself from staring at her buttocks, so round, so firm, at her narrow hips, at the taut bra-strap faintly visible through her jumper.

He felt suddenly giddy. He could not tell whether he was losing his balance or whether Valentine was swaying, grinding her hips almost imperceptibly in a still, silent, suggestive dance.

Antoine steadied himself on the doorframe. He needed air. He needed to get out. Right now.

He took the stairs four at a time, rushed to the kitchen sink, turned the water on full and plunged his face into his cupped hands. Then he shook himself, grabbed the tea towel and wiped his face.

As he set it down, he glimpsed the figure of Valentine in the hallway, heading for the door. The cold night air gusted into the room; Antoine began to run. Valentine was already out in the street, walking slowly and unhurriedly. She pushed open the gate of her parents' garden, calmly crossed it and went into the house, not bothering to close the door, so certain was she that Antoine was running after her.

Before he knew what had happened, he was in the Desmedts' house.

The characteristic smell of the place greeted him. It was a smell he had never liked, a combination of cabbage, sweat and wax polish.

Antoine took a step and stopped dead.

Directly in front of him, sitting at the far end of the long dining table, Monsieur Desmedt was staring at him.

All of a sudden he was convinced that the only reason Valentine had come over to his house was to bring him here to face her father.

The girl pretended to hang around, casually leafing through the T.V. guide, running a finger along the edge of the sideboard. Then she turned and stared at Antoine. She was a different person. The flighty teenager was once again consumed by the shadow of her little brother which floated in the room like a foreboding. She brusquely turned on her heel and went up the stairs and disappeared without a sign, without a backward glance.

"They're upstairs," Monsieur Desmedt said in a hollow voice.

He jerked his chin towards the upper floor from where garbled whispers could be heard. The living room was illuminated only by the bare bulb in the kitchen and the lights on the Christmas tree which were identical to their own. Probably bought from the same shop,

Antoine stood transfixed. A bottle of wine and an empty glass stood in front of Monsieur Desmedt. The man's head was bowed, he seemed thoughtful. He sat like this for a long moment, then abruptly seemed to remember that he was not alone. He nodded to the chair next to him. Antoine was terrified that the man would drag him from the doorway and force him to sit down. Nervously, he stepped forward. The more he approached, the closer he came, the more this brutal, hulking man terrified him.

"Take a seat."

The chair Antoine pulled out made a sound like chalk on a blackboard. Monsieur Desmedt stared at him for a long time.

"You know Rémi pretty well, don't you?"

Antoine pursed his lips slightly, yeah, pretty well, I mean, not very well . . .

"Can you imagine a kid like that running away? He's six years old."

Antoine shook his head.

"Can you imagine him wandering off into the back of beyond? Getting so lost he can't find his way home in a place where he was born and raised?"

Antoine realised that Monsieur Desmedt was not really asking questions, but voicing the thoughts he had been brooding over for hours. He said nothing.

"And why don't they keep looking for him through the night, huh? Surely they've got some bloody torches at the *gendarmerie?*"

Antoine made a helpless little gesture with his hands, unable to explain.

Monsieur Desmedt exuded an unpleasant smell which mingled with the wine he had obviously been drinking in some quantity.

"I should go." Antoine muttered.

When Monsieur Desmedt did not move, he slowly got to his feet as though he did not want to rouse him.

Then Monsieur Desmedt turned abruptly, grabbed him by the hips and pulled him close. He slipped his arms around Antoine's waist, pressed his face into the boy's chest and burst into tears.

Antoine almost toppled under the force, but managed to stay upright. He saw the thick, pale neck of Rémi's father racked by sobs, breathed in his overpowering odour.

Imprisoned in the man's brawny arms, Antoine wished that he could die.

On the sideboard there were family photos in ill-assorted

frames. One of them was empty, the one that had held the snapshot they had given to the *gendarmes*, the one that had been shown on television, Rémi in his yellow T-shirt, his unruly tuft of hair . . .

The other frames had not been rearranged to fill the gap. They were waiting for Rémi's photograph to return to its usual place, for life to return to normal.

9

Day seemed as though it would never break, the sky above the town loured a boundless milky white. The first to arrive found Monsieur Desmedt standing under the porch light, staring at his garden, wearing heavy boots and a beige parka, his balled fists stuffed into the pockets. He had the hard-faced expression of days best forgotten.

There were many more men than women, but there were also some bigger boys, older than Antoine, sixteen- and eighteen-year-olds he knew only vaguely.

Antoine had not closed his eyes all night, he was sapped of all strength.

The moment he looked out his bedroom window and saw the crowd gathered outside the Desmedts' house, preparing to set off for the *mairie*, his courage failed him.

"What d'you mean you're not coming?"

Madame Courtin was outraged. What would people think if he didn't come, what would the neighbours say about him, about them? Even if only for Bernadette's sake . . . The whole town was taking part in the search, it was their duty!

"The Mouchottes won't be going!" said Antoine.

It was a hypocritical argument, he knew it was; no-one hated the Desmedts more than the Mouchottes, people often said it was a good thing their houses were separated by the Courtins', because otherwise the two men would long since have ripped out each other's guts.

"That's different," Madame Courtin said, "you know perfectly well . . ."

To end the argument, Antoine conceded defeat and came downstairs.

He shook a few hands and tried to stay as far as possible from the Desmedt family, which was hardly difficult since they were surrounded by so many people. Valentine was still wearing her red jeans, but in the dreary light of dawn the colour seemed washed out while the girl, engulfed by the crowd, looked older, out of place, inconsequential.

They set off in procession towards the meeting point.

Although those flanking the Desmedts observed a respectful silence, further back, rumours were flying and tongues wagging. Firstly, the pond . . . I mean, honestly, for years they've been talking about putting up safety barriers, but have the *mairie* bothered to lift a finger . . . ?

And this search today, is it being run by the *mairie* or the *préfecture*?

The exceptional circumstances offered a new channel for the townspeople's fury, which had been simmering now for two days, they vented their anger at the *mairie*, meaning the mayor, meaning the proprietor of Weiser Wooden Toys. All the rancour stirred up by the various threats to the community coalesced into an inchoate rage which, finding no direct outlet, had been transferred onto this incident.

Two large white tents had been set up outside the *mairie* by the *sécurité civile*, the emergency services and the *gendarmes* were in attendance. Where are the search and rescue dogs? someone asked. Madame Courtin was talking to the grocer. Antoine tried to listen in, but he could not hear; there was a deep rumbling inside his head, an incessant vibration that muffled every sound, he caught a word here, a snatch of conversation there – Hey Antoine! He turned. It was Théo.

"You've no business being here!"

Antoine opened his mouth to speak, why should he have . . . The mayor's son puffed out his chest, happy to break the bad news.

"You have to be an adult to take part!" he said, as though he was not personally affected by this restriction.

Madame Courtin quickly turned to them.

"Is that true?"

A *gendarme* arrived, the one who had interviewed Antoine the night before.

"Participants must be at least sixteen years old." He gave the two boys a half smile. "It's good of you to volunteer, but . . ."

New arrivals joined the growing crowd. People shook hands, affected a self-effacing but resolute attitude. The mayor was chatting with *gendarmes* and members of the *sécurité civile*. Ordnance survey maps had been spread out. A police van arrived with four dogs tugging on their leashes. About bloody time! someone said.

It took some time to organise the groups, each of which was led by a *gendarme* or a member of the emergency services. Clear, firm instructions were issued. The men, wearing caps and woolly hats, nodded sagely.

Antoine counted a dozen groups of eight.

The television crew arrived, creating a buzz of excitement. A cameraman panned across the crowd of people anxious to appear orderly, willing and responsible. The reporter was spoiled for choice, everyone had something to say. A woman whom Antoine had never seen before was telling the journalist how distraught she was, clasping her hands to her chest, anyone would have sworn she was the missing boy's mother. While she was pouring her heart out, the reporter was standing on tiptoe, desperately scanning the crowd for Rémi's parents. When she at last located them, she did not even allow the woman to finish her sentence but elbowed a path through the crowd, followed by the cameraman, zigzagging towards the large white tent.

When Madame Desmedt saw them approach, she began to sob. The cameraman quickly shouldered his kit.

Within two hours, the footage he was shooting would be broadcast all around France.

Madame Desmedt's grief and what she said were gut-wrenching. Give him back. Three words, barely audible.

Give him back.

Her voice was anguished, tremulous.

The assembled crowd were so moved that one by one they fell silent as though in a silent prayer that some feared might be prophetic.

The young *gendarme*, armed with a megaphone, climbed the steps of the *mairie* while officers wearing armbands handed out leaflets.

"Thank you all for coming here this morning, especially on such a miserable day . . ."

Secretly everyone felt doubly virtuous and compassionate.

"We would you ask you to carefully read the instructions on the leaflets being distributed. Do not move too quickly, focus only on what is directly in front of you. It is crucial that every square metre we search can be definitively eliminated from our investigation. Do I make myself clear?"

There was a murmur of agreement.

While the *gendarme* was speaking, Antoine was distracted by the arrival of Madame Antonetti and the parish priest.

"There are nine groups. Four will go to the pond with the dog handlers, three will search the western perimeter of the woods, and the last two groups will head up towards Saint-Eustache."

Antoine froze. It was over. He had a shudder of relief.

Now he knew what would happen, he knew what he would do. In a way, it made things easier.

"After we break for lunch, we will assign new areas to each group, depending on the progress made this morning. If today's search should prove fruitless, we would request that you volunteer again tomorrow."

It was at this moment that Monsieur Kowalski appeared.

He moved with slow, faltering steps. People fell silent as he passed, everyone stood aside – not out of deference, but because the man reeked of brimstone. He's been released . . . the words were on everyone's lips. They looked at each other warily. Had he been released on bail? No-one had heard anything.

As Monsieur Kowalski approached the *mairie*, those he left in his wake began to mutter in low voices. He might have been released, but only for lack of evidence . . . after all, the police don't just make arrests at random, only if people are somehow involved in a case. No smoke without fire, Kowalski . . . they say his business is in financial difficulties, that he has to do the rounds of the neighbouring village markets just to make ends meet.

Kowalski's face betrayed no emotion, it was gaunt and wizened as ever, those hollow cheeks, those bushy eyebrows . . .

He passed close to Antoine and his mother. Madame Courtin pointedly turned her back on him. He approached the *gendarme*, stopped and spread his arms, I am here, tell me what you want from me.

The *gendarme* studied the various groups, felt their negative energy. People looked away, some turned their backs, the more uncompromising walked off without waiting for the signal.

"I see . . ." said the *gendarme*, with a hint of weariness. "Alright, you can come with us."

The crowd set off, conversations resumed, the ground was already strewn with the *sécurité civile* leaflets.

Back at home, Antoine stood at his bedroom window for a

long time, staring into the distance. When they found the body, they would radio the *préfecture*, he would see the flashing lights far away, heading up the dirt track to Saint-Eustache.

He closed the window and went into the bathroom.

He emptied everything from the medicine cabinet. Madame Courtin, like most of her compatriots, was a conspicuous consumer of medications; there were countless bottles each containing a small quantity of pills. Together, they made a huge pile of pills.

Suppressing the urge to retch, Antoine swallowed them in fistfuls. His face was streaked with tears.

10

In a sickening spasm, the tidal wave in his stomach ripped through his whole body, burned through his belly and exploded into his throat with a jolt that literally lifted him off the bed. He hung his head over the side, a guttural howl came from deep within his gut, a thin trickle of bile hung from his lips as he choked and gasped for breath.

He felt shattered, his back was in agony. With each fresh wave, his whole body roiled and churned, dissolving and liquefying as though determined to expel itself from his skin.

This went on for two long hours.

His mother came up regularly to check on him, to empty the basin on the rug beside the bed, wipe the corners of his mouth, dab his forehead with a cold compress and go back downstairs.

When the spasms finally subsided, Antoine drifted off to sleep.

In his dream, Rémi, like him, was exhausted, he had no energy left. Lying in the yawning black crevasse, he could no longer reach out his arms, only wave his tiny hands in a last desperate effort. Death was coming, it was here, it had grabbed his feet and was dragging him in, Rémi was sinking, disappearing . . .

Antoine!

When he woke, it was dark. He had no idea what time it was, but he knew it was not the middle of the night since the television downstairs was blaring. He listened for the church bell, whose peals reached him when the breeze blew in the right direction. There was a brisk wind whipping through the shutters. He thought he counted six chimes but could not be sure. He settled on somewhere between five and seven o'clock in the morning.

He looked at the nightstand. There was a glass of water and a jug. A bottle of some medication he did not recognise.

He heard the front door bell, the television clicked off.

A man's voice, then hushed whispering.

Then footsteps on the stairs and Docteur Dieulafoy appeared, alone, carrying his fat leather bag which he set down next to the bed. He bent over Antoine, laid a hand on his sweaty forehead for a moment then, without a word, took off his coat, extracted his stethoscope, threw back the sheet, pushed up his pyjama top (who had put his pyjamas on? He could not remember), and silently went about examining him, focusing on some imaginary, floating point.

Downstairs, the television had come on again, but the sound was turned down. The doctor took Antoine's pulse. Then he packed away his stethoscope and sat on the bed, his feet set apart, arms folded, looking pensive and circumspect.

Docteur Dieulafoy was about fifty years old. His father, everyone agreed, had been a Breton sailor who had travelled all over the world; as to his mother, there were various theories: a housemaid from Vietnam, a prostitute from China, some cheap hussy from Thailand . . . Rumours offered a very scant portrait of this woman about whom no-one actually knew anything.

The doctor had been living in the village for twenty-five years, and no-one could boast that they had ever seen him smile. He spent every day of the year driving the winding roads of the *canton*, saw patients at unseasonable hours, everyone knew him and had called on him at one time or another, he had been invited to dozens of weddings, communions and christenings, had attended the funerals of countless old people, and yet no-one knew anything about him. He had no wife, no children, the grocer's daughter cleaned house for him, while he took care of the surgery himself. On Sundays, whatever the weather, he threw open the surgery windows and, wearing a tattered old vest, could be seen dusting, hoovering and polishing, and if a passing patient should call, Docteur Dieulafoy would open his door, usher them inside, wash his hands, set down the duster and the wax polish, and hold an impromptu consultation.

Antoine propped himself up on his pillows. His stomach had stopped heaving at last, but it still ached and he had a lingering, acrid taste of vomit in his mouth.

The doctor sat, motionless, engrossed in his thoughts. His

broad, swarthy face was utterly inscrutable and his stillness was beginning to make Antoine uneasy, but after a moment, it was as though he were not there, as though he were simply a part of the furniture. Antoine became absorbed in his own thoughts. It had not worked. He had wanted to die but he had failed. He would have to explain, to justify himself. Suddenly he remembered the search parties setting out for Saint-Eustache ... There was nothing to explain anymore, he merely needed to confirm what everyone by now knew. The weight of the burden he had to bear was so overwhelming that he felt exhausted, and he closed his eyes and sank back into the pillows.

"Do you want to tell me about it, Antoine?"

The doctor's voice was barely audible. He had not moved a millimetre.

Antoine did not have the strength to answer. Rémi's death was both intensely present and terribly remote, his mind was a jumble of questions. What had they done with Rémi's body? He pictured Bernadette sitting next to the supine corpse, trying to warm the tiny hand in hers ...

Were they waiting for Docteur Dieulafoy to pronounce him medically fit before coming to arrest him? Were the *gendarmes* keeping his mother downstairs? Given that he was a minor, maybe only a doctor was allowed to hear his confession ... He had forgotten the question he had been asked.

The darkness of his bedroom made him feel closer to Rémi. It was a very dark place that they had taken him from.

He imagined the men peering beneath the fallen beech tree. Monsieur Desmedt would not allow anyone to fetch his son from the shadowy crevasse, even the paramedics would maintain a respectful distance. They would have brought a stretcher and a blanket with which to cover the body. The moment when Monsieur Desmedt pulled his son towards him was unendurable. He grabbed the boy by one arm and Rémi's head – that unmistakable shock of sandy hair – rose above the lip of the hole, followed by his shoulders. The body was so limp, so contorted that the limbs seemed to appear in no particular order.

Antoine began to cry.

He felt an unexpected rush of relief. The tears were not like those he had shed while he was still free, instead they came in a deep, soothing torrent. They were cleansing tears.

Docteur Dieulafoy nodded gravely, agreeing with something that had not been said but he seemed to understand.

Antoine's tears were inexhaustible. Inexplicably, the moment was tinged with happiness, with joy at this sense of a relief he had thought would never come. It was over, and his sobs were now those of a child, there was something protective about them, they offered a comfort that would remain with him wherever he was taken.

The doctor sat for a long time, listening to Antoine's sobbing, then he got up, snapped his bag shut, picked up his coat without looking at the boy.

And he left without a word.

Antoine calmed himself, blew his nose and sat up against his pillows. Perhaps he should get dressed before people arrived . . . He did not know what to do, this was the first time he had been arrested.

It was his mother's footsteps he heard echoing in the stairwell. So she was coming to get him dressed and bring him downstairs. He wished it could be someone else, his mother would cling to him as the *gendarmes* dragged him away.

Madame Courtin wrinkled her nose as she stepped into the room, the stench of vomit . . .

She picked up the basin and was about to set it outside on the landing, but then came back and, despite the gale blustering outside, she opened one of the shutters to let in some air. The chill wind rushed into the room Antoine noticed his mother's forehead was lined by a small furrow, a sign that she was worried about something.

She turned to her son.

"Are you feeling a little better?"

Without waiting for an answer, she picked up the medicine bottle from the nightstand and poured a teaspoon.

"It was that roast capon that did for you . . . I had to throw the thing out. I mean really, people shouldn't be allowed to sell meat in that state."

Antoine did not react.

"Here, take this," she said. "It's for indigestion, it'll make you feel better."

This reference to a minor ailment made him wonder and worry. Warily, he swallowed the medicine. He was not sure he understood what was happening. Madame Courtin put the cap back on the bottle.

"I've made some broth, I'll bring you up a bowl."

She had been talking about the capon, but as far as he could remember he had barely touched it. And besides, if he was suffering from a stomach upset, why was his mother not ill too? After all, she had eaten the same meal.

Antoine tried to recall the sequence of events, but a lot of things were muddled in his head. He could not distinguish between what was real and what he had dreamed. He got up. His legs were weak, he stumbled and had to sit on the bed. He thought about Valentine. Had she been part of his dream, or had she been real? He saw her standing in front of him while he tried to tie his laces, saw himself trying to get up quickly and falling back on the bed, just like now.

There had been Christmas Eve, and Monsieur Desmedt with his arms around his waist. And then the search parties sent out to scour the woods and the area around Saint-Eustache . . .

He closed his eyes and waited for the dizzy spell to pass, then tried again. Leaning against the wall and the furniture for support, he stumbled out onto the landing, opened the bathroom door and, propping himself against the toilet, opened the medicine cabinet.

Empty.

He clearly remembered pills scattered over his nightstand before he fell asleep, some had even landed on the floor . . . Where were they now?

With difficulty he made his way back to his room.

It was a relief to be able to lie down.

"Here you go . . ."

Madame Courtin had brought up a tray with a steaming

bowl of broth which she set down carefully on the bed.

"I don't feel that hungry," Antoine said weakly.

"I'm not surprised, that's always the way with a stomach upset, you can feel peaky for ages, you don't feel like eating."

The television blaring in the living room worried Antoine. Madame Courtin was not in the habit of having the T.V. on in the middle of the morning, in fact it went against her principles. Staring at that screen makes people stupid!

"Docteur Dieulafoy said he'd come by again this evening to check you're alright. I told him not to bother, I mean, obviously you're fine, we're hardly going to make a big fuss over a little tummy upset. But he insisted – you know what he's like, that man, so conscientious . . . So, anyway, he'll be back later . . ."

Madame Courtin was poking around the room, going from the chest of drawers to the window, pointlessly opening and closing doors, trying to busy herself, to seem composed, but her obvious unease belied the firm, confident voice with which she said:

"I mean, would you credit it! Selling me a capon that's gone off! Oh, he'll be hearing about this from me, let me tell you!"

Antoine noticed that she avoided using Monsieur Kowalski's name. This was just like her, if you did not talk about something, that something did not exist.

"Anyway," Madame Courtin went on, "a little tummy upset is hardly worth making a song and dance about. That's what I said to Docteur Dieulafoy, he was prattling on about hospital and blah, blah, blah, but in the end he gave you something to make you vomit and that was that."

It was as though she wanted him to back up her story.

"An emetic, they call it, apparently. News to me . . . So you don't fancy any of this broth, then?"

After this long rigmarole that Antoine had not really understood, Madame Courtin seemed suddenly in a hurry to leave.

"Want me to turn off the light? You should get some rest . . . Sleep, now that's the best medicine."

She switched off the light and pulled the door to after her.

In the dim bedroom all that could be heard was the whistle of the wind as it grew stronger. Perhaps a storm was brewing.

Antoine tried to make sense of everything he had seen and heard, the doctor's visit, his mother's ramblings . . . What did it all mean?

He fell asleep.

He was woken by the ringing of the doorbell.

He did not know whether he had been dozing or whether he had been asleep for hours. He threw off the blankets, went and stood by the half-open window, and then he recognised the doctor's voice.

Madame Courtin was whispering.

"Wouldn't it be better to just let him sleep?"

But then the doctor's footsteps on the stairs.

Antoine got back into bed, rolled onto his side and closed his eyes.

The doctor came into the room and stood motionless by

the bed for a long moment. Antoine anxiously tried to regulate his breathing. How do you breathe when you're asleep? He adopted a long, slow rhythm that he thought matched a sleeper's breathing.

After a while the doctor stepped forward and sat in the same spot on the bed as he had on his first visit.

Antoine could hear his own heartbeat and the howling wind outside.

"If you're worried about anything, Antoine . . ."

He spoke in a quiet, calm, confiding tone. Antoine had to listen hard to understand.

". . . you can call me any time. Day or night. You can come and see me, you can phone, whatever you like . . . You're bound to feel weak for a day or two, then things will start to get back to normal and maybe when that happens, you'll want to talk to someone . . . Nobody's going to force you, it's just that . . ."

The words came slowly, the doctor's sentences did not end but simply faded in the room like an insubstantial vapour.

"If I'd admitted you to hospital . . . things would have been very different, you realise . . . But now, as things stand, well, I don't really know how to . . . And that's why I came round to tell you that, whatever happens, I mean, if something happens, you can come to me, you can call me . . . any time. That's all. Just to talk. Any time at all."

Neither Antoine nor anyone else in the village had ever heard Docteur Dieulafoy speak at such length.

He sat in silence for a while to allow Antoine, if he were

listening, time to take in what he was saying, and then he got up and left as he had come. Like an apparition.

Antoine could not comprehend it. Docteur Dieulafoy had not spoken to him, he had whispered a lullaby. He did not change his position. He lay there and let himself be carried away by sleep, forcing himself to ignore the wailing of the wind as it echoed in his bedroom: the harrowing cry of a thousand voices . . .

Antoine!

When he woke again he was certain that it was late, even though downstairs the television was still on.

The events of the day before came back to him in all their clarity. The search parties setting out, the pills, the doctor's visit . . .

He should have run away.

Another memory comes back to him: he had wanted to run away.

He got up, he felt weak but he could stand. He knelt and groped under his bed. Nothing. Though he was certain – absolutely certain – that he had shoved his rucksack full of clothes there. And the shirt he had screwed into a ball.

He leapt to his feet and searched through the chest of drawers: everything was back in its place. His Spiderman action figure had been placed on top of the globe. He opened the drawers of his desk. The papers he had hidden there were gone.

He needed to be sure in his own mind.

He opened the door of his room a chink and silently tiptoed

down the stairs. He could hear the soft voices of the television. He crept into the hall and, screwing up his face, he opened the top drawer of the console table. His passport and the Travel Authorisation for a Minor were right there, exactly where they had been ...

He was convinced his mother had cleared the pills from the nightstand, unpacked the rucksack he obviously intended to use in his escape, replaced his passport and his savings book ...

Why did she think Antoine wanted to run away? How much did she actually know? Probably nothing. But she had probably deduced the essentials. Did she suspect that Antoine was linked to Rémi's disappearance?

He closed the drawer, took one step, then another. Peering in, he saw his mother in front of the television, her chair pulled up to the screen like a blind woman. She was watching the midnight news on the local channel. The sound was turned down so low as to be barely audible:

". . . of the child who disappeared on Thursday afternoon. Regrettably, a search of woodland areas near the town turned up no new evidence. It proved impossible for the search parties to comb the area where the child might have strayed to in a single day, in particular the woods near Saint-Eustache, and therefore the *gendarmerie* has a second multi-agency search planned for tomorrow morning."

Footage showed lines of people walking shoulder to shoulder, slowly and deliberately.

"The initial focus of the *sécurité civile*, a pond near Beauval, is being dragged by divers who will resume their search tomorrow."

Seeing his mother hunched anxiously next to the television made Antoine's stomach lurch and once again he wished he could die.

"Witnesses are requested to call the Freephone number at the bottom of the screen. Just a reminder that, when he disappeared, six-year-old Rémi Desmedt was wearing . . ."

Antoine crept back up to his room.

One day had not been enough for them to scour the woods, a second search had been scheduled. For tomorrow morning.

They would go back.

For Antoine, there would be no second chance.

He wished that the storm, which had been threatening for the past two days, would finally break.

Outside the wind lashed harder, rattling the shutters on their hinges.

11

The gale continued to gain in strength throughout the night, becoming so fierce that, by the early hours, the torrential downpour dwindled as the rain-swollen clouds were forced to admit defeat.

Across the landscape, the storm left the dramatic scar of its passage. Rather than waning, as had been expected, it laid siege to the region like an invader confident of his superior power.

The whole town was awake.

Antoine felt the weight of the exhaustion that had accumulated over the past two days, especially as he had not slept a wink.

He had spent the night imagining what form it would take, this catastrophe that was now inevitable. He lay on his bed and listened to the storm rage. Behind the closed shutters the windowpanes clattered, wind gusted into the chimney making a dull roar. He felt there was a confused correlation between this house as it shuddered beneath the force of the gale and his own life. He also spent a lot of time thinking about his mother.

She knew nothing specific about Antoine's role in the disappearance of Rémi; anyone else would be plagued by gruesome images, by the sheer horror, but Madame Courtin had her own way of dealing with things. Between the facts she found disturbing and her imagination, she built a thick wall that filtered out everything but an inchoate dread that she could mollify thanks to an extraordinary list of habits and mysterious rituals. Life always triumphs in the end, this was a favourite expression. It meant that life must go on, not as it is, but as she might wish it to be. Reality was simply a matter of willpower, it was pointless to allow oneself to be overwhelmed by trivial worries, the easiest way to be rid of them was to ignore them, it was a flawless approach, her whole life was proof that it worked perfectly.

Her son had tried to kill himself by swallowing the contents of the medicine cabinet, fine, that was one way of seeing things. But if you considered it as a tummy upset brought on by a capon from Monsieur Kowalski, tragedy was reduced to a minor setback, a bad patch to get through, two days sipping broth and everything would be fine.

Antoine's thoughts were difficult to dissociate from the murky half-light, from the noise of the wind, shrieking like some colossal engine, that threatened to topple the house.

He decided to go downstairs. He wondered whether his mother had been to bed. She was wearing the same clothes as on the day before. In the living room the television was still on, the sound turned down as low as possible.

The breakfast she had made, the table laid with plates and cutlery, were just the same as every morning, but she had not opened the shutters, it was like having breakfast in the middle of the night, the wind whipping through the slats set the ceiling light swinging.

"I wasn't able to get them open."

She looked at her son in terror. She had not said good morning, had not asked how he was feeling . . .

She was astonished that she had not been able to open the shutters. There was an anxious tone in her voice. The weather forecast announcing serious storm damage would not be appeased by a bowl of broth . . .

"Maybe you'll manage better than me."

Antoine knew that this request masked a number of others that he did not quite understand.

He went to the window, turned the handle, and the window flew open with such force that he almost fell over backwards. Only by leaning all his weight on the handle did he manage to get it closed again.

"Probably best to wait till it dies down."

He sat down to breakfast. He knew his mother would ask him no questions, she was busy buttering a *biscotte* the way she always did, the jam was in its usual place on the table. Antoine was not hungry. After a few minutes of a silent conversation that exemplified their mutual incomprehension, he cleared away his plate and went back to his room.

The PlayStation had been packed away in its box. He

took it out and started a game, but still he felt anxious.

When he heard the television downstairs being turned up, he went onto the landing and cautiously went down a few steps. A severe thunderstorm warning had been issued with strong-gale force winds expected over the coming hours. People were advised to remain indoors.

What they were experiencing now was just the beginning. Confirmation of the forecast came less than an hour later.

The windows shook like leaves, the wind whistled through every crack, the whole house echoed with ominous groans and creaks.

Concerned, Madame Courtin went up to the attic, but did not stay there for more than five minutes. The roof tiles rattled, several leaks had sprung and water trickled down the walls and onto the floor. When she reappeared she was deathly pale.

At the first loud crash, she started and let out a scream. It came from somewhere to the north of the house.

"Stay here," Antoine said. "I'll go and check it out."

He slipped on his parka and his shoes. Madame Courtin would have tried to stop him, but she was petrified with fear, she did not realise the danger he was in until he opened the door. She shouted to him but it was too late, he had already pulled the door shut, he was outside.

The cars parked along the road had begun to slalom ominously. Thunder growled like a vicious dog about to attack, a continual barrage of lightning bolts strobed the houses with a bluish light, some of the roofs were beginning to shear.

On the far side of the street, two telegraph poles were

lying one on top of the other. Whipped up by the wind, a jumbled wreckage of tarpaulins, buckets, and wooden boards hurtled past, close enough to touch. A yowl of fire engines could just be heard, but it was impossible to tell where they were headed.

The wind was powerful enough to toss Antoine to the far end of the garden and indeed beyond. He had to try and cling to something solid, but looking at the cars and the rooftops, it was obvious that nothing could be considered solid under these conditions. Bent double, he crawled, hand over hand, to get to the other side of the house. He glanced around a corner and barely had time to duck as a whirling sheet of corrugated iron flew past, narrowly missing his head. He was on his knees, keeping his head as low as possible and shielding himself with his arms.

The fir tree had fallen across the garden. A fir tree that was almost ten years old, planted one Christmas, Antoine remembered photographs of the family gathered for the ceremony – his father had still been living with them at the time.

The whole village seemed to buckle, warping and bending as though about to be uprooted.

Antoine stood up, dropping his guard only for a moment, but this was enough for a mighty gust to lift him off his feet. He landed almost a metre away, scrabbled for something to hold on to, but he was struggling against an overpowering force, he rolled over and over until he was slammed against the garden wall. He huddled against it, his head between his knees. He could barely breathe.

The task of making it back to the front door seemed hopeless.

Seeing the Desmedts' house reminded him that a second search had been scheduled for that morning. By now everyone should have been heading towards Saint-Eustache, but no-one was outdoors, it would have been impossible to walk as far as the end of the street.

He crawled to the fence that separated their garden from the Desmedts' and peered through the slats. The swing set had toppled onto the grass. Everything else had been blown away and was lying against the far wall. Including the rubbish sacks. The bag containing Ulysses had burst. The dog's corpse protruded from the ripped plastic, a mass of dark, blood-spattered fur. Antoine stared in horror, then turned back towards his own house. The satellite dish mounted on the corner was swaying dangerously.

But for the fact that his mother would worry if he did not come back, he would gladly have stayed there huddled against the low wall, watching as, piece by piece, the house was swept away.

Finally he laid himself flat on the ground to give the wind as little purchase as possible, and he crawled. Crossing the garden like this took him several minutes. He managed to get around to the other side of the house and enter by the back door, which was a little more sheltered. By the time he got inside, he was exhausted.

His mother rushed to him and hugged him. She was breathless, as though she was the one who had been outside braving the storm.

"My God! How could I let you go out in such weather!"

It was impossible to know when the gales would subside. By now it had stopped raining, the storm had passed, there was only the wind which raged on, growing harder and faster with every passing minute.

With the windows and the shutters closed, they lived blindly, like people under siege, listening to the house creak like a ship tossed on stormy seas. At 11.00 a.m., the television sputtered out, the satellite dish had probably been ripped away. An hour later it was the electricity. The telephone line was dead too.

Madame Courtin sat in the kitchen, her hands cradling a mug of cold coffee. Antoine felt unexpectedly protective, he did not want to leave her alone so he came and sat beside her. They did not talk. His mother's face was so ashen that he felt an urge to lay his hand on hers, but he held back, not knowing what doors such a gesture might open, given the circumstances . . .

He knew there was a chink in the living-room shutters through which he could look out at the street. He was stunned by what he saw. The two cars that had been there earlier were gone, a tree several metres high was rolling down the road at terrifying speed, smashing into walls and gates. The peak of the storm lasted for three hours.

Towards 4.00 p.m., calm was restored.

People could hardly believe it. Doors and windows were opened warily, one after another.

The inhabitants of Beauval stood speechless and surveyed

the damage wreaked by this storm that German meteorologists had named "Lothar".

But soon they were forced to retreat indoors again.

The rain that had ceased while the storm was at its height now returned, claiming its right to add to the devastation.

12

The rains lashed Beauval with such terrifying force that, within minutes, the sky turned black. Since the wind had completely died away, the ropes of water fell vertically. The streets quickly flooded to become streams and then roaring rivers, sweeping away everything tossed there by the winds some hours earlier – dustbins, letterboxes, crates, planks, even a small white dog that struggled to stay afloat and was found crushed against a wall the next day. Cars that, hours earlier, had been whipped away by the storm now floated in the other direction, eddying on the floodwaters.

Antoine heard something falling in the cellar, he opened the door and flicked the switch, but the electricity was still out.

"Don't go down there, Antoine," Madame Courtin said.

But he had already grabbed the flashlight that hung on the wall and had descended the first few steps. The sight before him took his breath away: the water was more than a metre deep, everything that was not screwed down was floating: camping gear, boxes of clothes, suitcases ...

He stumbled back up and slammed the door behind him. "We need to go upstairs," he said.

They had to organise themselves because if the water reached the ground floor, as it threatened to do, there was no way of knowing when they would be able to come down again. While the wind hammered on the door as though trying to break in, Madame Courtin rapidly gathered together some provisions and set them on the stairs together with all those items she considered precious – her handbag, the photograph albums, a shoebox full of official documents, a pot plant (why that particular one was a mystery), a crocheted cushion given to her by her mother – it looked as though she was planning to take part in the Exodus. Antoine went from room to room turning off all the electrical appliances. The water was rising at a spectacular rate. It began to spill out from under the cellar door, stream across the floor and flood into every room. By the time they had carried everything upstairs, it had risen by two or three centimetres, it seemed as though nothing would stop it.

Antoine sat on the stairs. The floodwater had just passed the first step and was still rising. Bobbing on its surface came the sofa cushions, the T.V. guide, a book of crossword puzzles, some empty boxes, the plastic broom from the kitchen . . .

The situation was becoming nerve-wracking. They could hide out upstairs, but would that be enough? He remembered seeing television programmes about floods where the water reached the rooftops and people were forced to cling on to their chimneys. Would that happen to them?

The storm returned, thunder boomed above their heads as

though it were in the same room, blinding flashes lit up the windows. Still the rain fell, still the waters rose.

Antoine went to join his mother. Now that the wind had begun to subside, Madame Courtin was going through the first-floor rooms, opening all the shutters.

Through the windows, they discovered a new landscape. Patios, gardens, pavements were all submerged beneath a mass of water thirty centimetres deep, gushing along the main street at terrifying speed, a swirling muddy river that had burst its banks. The storm had wreaked havoc on the roofs, ripping away hundreds of tiles.

What sort of state would their roof be in? Antoine looked up: the ceiling had changed colour, it was darker and here and there fat drops were beginning to bead. He began to wonder whether the whole house might not cave in onto their heads. But it was impossible to leave. Through the bedroom window he saw the supermarket delivery van float past, followed by another vehicle, as though a dam had just burst somewhere, the Peugeot belonging to the Mouchottes whirled by like a spinning top, colliding with a wall, then crashing into a road sign that buckled on impact. A few minutes later the mayor's official car appeared, tossed on the roiling torrent and, in its wake, the railings from outside the *mairie*.

Madame Courtin began to sob. Like him, she was probably afraid, but mostly she was weeping for the world she had always known which was disappearing before her eyes at an alarming speed. The townspeople doubtless saw this cataclysm as an ordeal sent to try them personally.

Instinctively, Antoine put an arm around his mother's shoulders, but to no avail. Madame Courtin had dissociated, horrified and spellbound by the roaring torrent surging along the street, crushing, destroying, sparing nothing. Antoine was shocked to watch a surreal procession of items of furniture from the ground floor of the school floating past, as though they had dived into the water like synchronised swimmers. The flood loomed over his life, annexing it.

And then he thought of Rémi.

The water would rise and rise, it would reach the brow of the hill, flood the woods of Saint-Eustache, it would disentomb Rémi, his body would float free from its hiding-place. In a matter of minutes, the whole town would watch as Rémi's corpse glided through the streets like a ghost, floating on his back, arms splayed, mouth open, only to be recovered several kilometres away . . .

Antoine was too exhausted now for tears.

They sat there for a long time. Every so often, Antoine would check to see how much the water had risen downstairs. By now it had reached the top of the dining-room table.

Then, slowly but surely, the storm began to move on.

At about 3.00 p.m., heavy rain was still falling over Beauval, but it was nothing compared to the cloudburst they had experienced all morning. Antoine and his mother could not go downstairs since the ground floor was submerged beneath more than a metre of water. The ceilings dripped, the mattresses were sodden, there was no escape from the wetness. It was beginning to get cold. Marooned with no electricity, no telephone, they were survivors waiting to be rescued.

The *sécurité civile* helicopter made a single reconnaissance flight over Beauval and was not seen again. The town was abandoned to its fate, the inhabitants trapped in their houses.

Night fell on a desolate landscape, although Antoine and his mother could see only the small patch framed by their bedroom windows.

The streetlights did not come on, but by eight o'clock they could make out that the waters were beginning to subside. The turbulent torrent in the street had abated considerably. Downstairs, the floodwater was beginning to drain away. But a strange whiff of doom still hung in the air as the squalls that had given way to the rain now returned, determined to have the last word.

As the waters seeped away, the wind blew harder. Once more they could feel the house judder on its foundations, the doors bulge and buckle as though pushed by some giant hand.

The howling gale grew louder, an angry rumbling of chimneys, windows and doors. Antoine and his mother barely had time to rush around, closing the first-floor shutters once more. A second storm was about to follow on from the first.

A few short hours after Lothar came the cyclone they named "Martin".

Of the two, this was the more violent, the more destructive.

The roofs that had been ripped open were now utterly swept away; the cars mired by the raging waters began to career dangerously, propelled by fierce flurries, some of which gusted at two hundred kilometres per hour.

Madame Courtin huddled in a corner of her bedroom, drawing her head into her shoulders. She looked so painfully fragile that Antoine was distraught. Once again he realised that he could never do anything to hurt her.

He came and huddled next to her, and they stayed that way all through the night.

13

At dawn, the town awoke in a state of shock. One by one doors opened, one by one the inhabitants poked out their heads, then emerged, distraught and petrified.

Though still exhausted, Madame Courtin went downstairs to survey the damage. The ground floor was entirely covered in a thick layer of mud, the furniture sodden, along the walls a horizontal line more than a metre above the floor indicated the high-water mark, the whole house reeked of sludge, but what could be done? There was still no electricity, no telephone . . . There was an eerie calm, as though time were suspended, and there was something in the air that signalled that the worst was over. Like the other townspeople, Madame Courtin felt it. Antoine saw her stand tall. She cleared her throat, moved with a more confident gait. She went outside, saw the fir tree that had fallen, took a few steps away from the house and looked up at the roof. Then she asked Antoine to go to the *mairie* to see whether they were entitled to aid.

Antoine pulled on his coat, slipped on his shoes and waded

through the waterlogged garden. Though it was not the first thought that occurred to him, when he looked at it more closely, it was plain to see that he and his mother were among the lucky ones, their roof had been miraculously spared, and while a number of tiles had been dislodged and some had fallen off and shattered, the damage was minimal.

The Desmedts had been less fortunate. Their chimney, blown over by a strong gust of wind, had crashed through the roof and the succeeding floors, taking bedrooms, bathroom and half of the kitchen with it and ending up in the cellar.

Swaddled in a dressing gown under a parka that was much too big for her, Bernadette was standing outside, staring up at the damage. As it ripped through the house, the chimney had destroyed the bed in Rémi's room. It was sickening to think that the little boy might have been asleep there, that the ceiling might have collapsed on him . . . He would have been killed instantly. Dazed by the scale of the tragedy that had overtaken her in the past two days, Bernadette now seemed utterly numb. Her thin frame resembled a piece of flotsam.

Monsieur Desmedt appeared at the window of Rémi's bedroom, he too looked stunned, as though he had come to wake his son and found him missing.

Valentine came down the front steps and joined her mother in the garden. She was dressed in the clothes she had been wearing the last time Antoine had seen her, but the red jeans and white leatherette jacket looked grubby, as though she had spent the night in a fight with someone. She was pale and dishevelled, a tartan shawl that probably belonged to her mother was thrown over her shoulders, her mascara had run, leaving darks streaks on her face. Antoine did not know where the image came from, but in this apocalyptic setting, the sexy, super-confident teenager of the night before now looked like a kid sent out to work the streets.

On the other side, the shutters had been ripped from the Mouchottes' house, the conservatory had collapsed and the garden was littered with shattered roof tiles and shards of glass as big as dinner plates.

Antoine saw Émilie's face pressed against the window, he gave her a little wave but she did not respond. She was staring at a spot in the middle of the road. Framed by the window, frozen and impassive, she looked like a girl in a Renaissance painting.

Her parents were already bustling about. Monsieur Mouchotte, his movements jerky as a robot, was filling rubbish sacks with the debris on the lawn. His wife, whom Antoine had always thought stunningly beautiful, was tugging at Émilie's sleeve, as though there was something unseemly about staring out of the window.

Walking through the centre, Antoine was met by a town that looked as though it had been bombed to rubble.

Not a single car was in its place, they had all been swept away by the gale-force winds to the outskirts of Beauval and now lay, a heap of misshapen metal, by the pillars of the railway bridge spanning the road. Lighter vehicles – scooters, motor-cycles and bicycles – were strewn everywhere, later they were found in cellars, under cars, in gardens, in the river. Shop windows had imploded and the storm had rushed in and littered the town with sodden packages from the chemist's, broken tools and fancy goods from Monsieur Lemercier's tobacconist's. Homeowners who had lost only forty or fifty tiles considered themselves lucky, since other houses had no roofs at all.

A crane in a building site had toppled onto the communal wash house, reducing the fifteenth-century façade to rubble. In their gardens or gravel driveways, people found a baby's crib, a doll, a bridal veil, small objects that God seemed to have placed there to prove that He could be whimsical in his mysterious ways. The young priest (doubtless busy explaining to his flocks all over the *département* that what was happening to them was a "Good Thing" – no easy task in the circumstances) would realise when He came again that God might be profoundly sensitive, but He also had a sense of irony: the church had been spared save for the rose window, where all the panes of stained glass had been smashed but for one, which depicted Saint Christopher, the patron saint of gales and thunderstorms.

The plane tree outside the *mairie*, uprooted by the storm, had fallen across the main street, crushing a van and separating the town into two equally ravaged zones. A caravan carried on the torrent from the municipal campsite had crashed into the *mairie* and the pavement was cluttered with plastic cutlery, mattresses, cupboard doors, bedside lamps, cushions and provisions.

Outside the *mairie* Antoine encountered a dozen people who had also come in search of aid. Each, as they itemised the damage they had suffered, claimed to be the worst affected; some had young children, or elderly parents in need of shelter, others insisted their house was about to collapse. All of them were right.

Monsieur Weiser came down from the mayoral office clutching a sheaf of papers and looking harried. Théo trailed after him. Out in the square he addressed the little group, attempting to explain things they did not want to hear: the emergency services were overwhelmed, and besides, it was impossible to call them since the telephone lines were down. The *préfecture* and the E.D.F. would certainly have put emergency procedures in place to restore the electricity, but there was no way of knowing whether this would take hours or days ... The group began to protest loudly.

"We need to get organised," the mayor shouted, brandishing the sheaf of paper. "First, we need to draw up an inventory of basic needs. The town council will collate all submissions and prioritise them." Under these circumstances, he fell back on administrative jargon intended to express proficiency with a strong emphasis on voluntarism.

"The gym has suffered only minor damage. Our first priority should be to set up a shelter for those who are home-less, a soup kitchen to feed everyone, we need to find blankets and bedding ..."

Monsieur Weiser spoke in a firm, determined voice. Given the all-encompassing chaos, the platitudes he trotted out took on the reassuring and familiar contours of familiar tasks.

"In order to restore the flow of traffic in Beauval, the plane tree will need to be chopped up and removed," he went on. "And for all of this we need manpower. Lots of manpower. Those with problems that can wait need to help out those in dire need."

Madame Kernevel appeared, looking very troubled.

"Maître Vallenères is lying in his garden," she announced. "He's dead. A falling tree!"

"Are . . . are you sure?"

As if the material damage were not enough, now there were fatalities.

"Oh, absolutely sure. I tried shaking him but he didn't move, and he's not breathing . . ."

An image flashed into Antoine's mind of Rémi lying dead. He remembered his own attempts to resuscitate the child.

"We need to go to him right now," the mayor said. "We need to carry him into his house."

He paused. No doubt to think about the measures he should take if the emergency services were indefinitely delayed. How would they deal with a dead body? Or with several bodies? Where could they be stowed?

"Who's going to look after his daughter?" someone asked.

Monsieur Weiser rubbed his bald pate.

Meanwhile, more people had arrived, including two of the town councillors who took up position behind the mayor. Several voices suggested setting up a shelter, they knew where to get hold of blankets, someone volunteered to open the gym. A tentative solidarity began to evolve. Monsieur Weiser announced a meeting to be held in the council chamber in one hour, all were welcome to attend, and decisions would be made . . .

From the back of the crowd came a loud voice. All heads turned.

"What about my son?" Monsieur Desmedt bellowed. "Who's going to help me find my son?"

He hung back from the group, arms dangling helplessly, fists clenched. What was striking was that there was none of the fury one might have expected of him. Instead it was a wail of sheer anguish.

"Weren't we supposed to be doing another search this morning?"

His voice faltered in its intensity, in its tone. His question was like that of a man who has lost his way and is asking for directions.

None of those who had taken part in the search organised by the *gendarmerie* the previous evening felt any less sympathetic to Monsieur Desmedt's plight, but there was such a yawning disparity between what he was suggesting and the devastating reality that extended as far as the eye could see that no-one had the heart to try to explain.

Monsieur Weiser, to whom the responsibility fell, coughed to clear his throat only to be interrupted by a firm, clear voice.

"Do you have any idea of the seriousness of the situation, Roger?"

Everyone turned.

Monsieur Mouchotte stood with his arms folded, assuming the pose of the pedant that he was. Émilie's father was a man who kept a high horse permanently saddled. Before being laid off he had been a tiresome foreman, pernickety, never given to generosity or indulgence. Standing a few metres away, he stared down Monsieur Desmedt, his bosom enemy. Everyone was remembering the resounding slap Rémi's father had given him back when they worked together, they remembered Monsieur Mouchotte reeling back and slumping in a box of wood shavings, gales of laughter only serving to add to his humiliation. Monsieur Weiser had suspended the guilty party for two days, but refused to fire him. Like everyone else, he probably thought the incident comic rather than actually violent, a comeuppance that was long overdue.

"All lines of communication are cut off," Monsieur Mouchotte said. "The town is in ruins, whole families are out on the streets. Who do you think you are to assume that your problems should take priority?"

His words were absolutely true, appallingly unfair, and entirely motivated by a desire for revenge so despicable that people's hearts sank. Even Antoine felt like leaping to Monsieur Desmedt's defence.

In normal circumstances, Monsieur Desmedt would have hurled himself at his enemy and others would have had to prise him off. But today there was no such need; Monsieur Desmedt did not lift a finger. This was precisely the response he had expected, and the fact that it had been delivered in such a shameful manner made little difference.

"Come now . . ." the mayor began feebly, but then words failed him.

It was not simply the fact that they were unable to help Desmedt that left them choked up, but the thought that the disappearance of his little boy, however tragic, had been relegated as a secondary concern and, swept away by this catastrophe that had affected everyone, would never again be something that concerned them all.

They could not carry on searching for the child; they accepted that he was gone for ever. Had he lost his way, had he been alive in the terrible hours of the storm, he would not be alive now.

Their only hope was that he had been kidnapped . . .

For Monsieur Desmedt, the ensuing silence foreshadowed the empty solitude that would henceforth mark his life.

Happy to have scored a victory, however dishonourable, Monsieur Mouchotte walked up to the mayor and offered his services, if there was *anything* he could do to help, in any capacity . . .

On his way home, Antoine tried to find supplies that could be used to clean up the house, a flashlight, maybe some batteries. He had no money with him, although in the circumstances, he could surely ask for credit, but the metal shutters on the ironmonger's shop were closed. Then, in a flash of inspiration, he thought of going to get some candles from the church.

As he went inside, he bumped into Madame Antonetti carrying a huge shopping bag. She glowered at him contemptuously.

There was not a single candle left in the holders.

14

The twin cyclones, the thunderstorm, the torrential rains had caused such a shockwave that, in Antoine's mind, everything that had gone before had faded. Only a few hours earlier he had been terrified that Rémi's body would float from the crevasse in Saint-Eustache and be carried through the town by the torrent; he had seen the child, floating on his back like a dead fish, drift past Antoine's house, past his parents' house . . . But this was not to happen. Though undeniably dramatic, the damage wreaked by the storm offered Antoine an unexpected reprieve. The body might be found kilometres from Beauval, the rains would have washed away much of the evidence.

Or it was simply a postponement and, a few days from now, the searches would begin again. If it was still where he had left it, Rémi's body was not so carefully hidden that a second search could miss it.

Antoine's fate was now governed by a deep uncertainty, a chance he began to cling to.

Madame Courtin had already begun to scrub the house

armed with a mop and a dozen floorcloths, a Sisyphean task. Antoine told her about the measures being taken by the *mairie*, none of which would have any positive impact on their situation.

"They don't care about people like us!" she said.

"Maître Vallenères is dead."

"Really? What happened?"

Madame Courtin stopped what she was doing and turned, still holding the mop over the bucket.

"A tree fell on him, apparently."

Madame Courtin returned to her scrubbing, though more slowly now. She was one of those people who struggled to juggle thinking with other activities.

"And his little girl, what's going to become of her?"

Antoine felt a pang of sympathy at the thought of the emaciated little girl. Who would push her wheelchair down the aisle at Sunday Mass? Who would take her out on summer afternoons, wheeling her through the town centre, stopping in front of the shops she never entered, buying her an ice cream which she would eat solemnly, sitting with the other customers on the terrace of the Café de Paris?

Usually, change in Beauval came slowly, evolution was gradual. The swiftness and savagery of events over the past three days had caught the townspeople unawares, the landscape was changing fast, too fast.

Antoine thought again about Monsieur Weiser. Like most people, he had little time for the mayor, but he thought about his efforts to mobilise the handful of available volunteers.

Despite the circumstances Monsieur Weiser had focused all his energies on the community even though – as he would find out later that day – the roof had been blown off his factory, and urgent measures would have to be taken to safeguard the machines, protect the stock, salvage as much as possible. He would have been completely justified in thinking about himself, like most of the inhabitants.

Given that their house was still standing and they still had a roof, thought Antoine, surely they should go and help the Desmedts.

"Do you honestly think I've nothing better to do?" his mother snapped with shocking thoughtlessness.

In the early afternoon, before a crowd of silent spectators, a chainsaw was taken to the plane tree outside the *mairie*. Some wondered how old it was, it had been there longer than anyone in Beauval could remember. The town square now looked like a barren desert. Meanwhile the roads around Beauval were littered with a veritable forest of fallen trees that prevented the workmen from carrying out repairs. For the next two days, communication with the outside world was fitful. Eventually, the electricity and later the telephone lines were restored.

The Courtin house stank of river mud, all the furniture would need to be replaced. People began to fill out insurance claims, submit requests to the *département* which promised speedy emergency funds; they were slow in coming, and for the most part did not arrive at all. Blanche Courtin worked like a Trojan, silent, focused, but she was irritated by the slightest thing, her manner and her reactions were brusque and brutal.

Antoine, together with Théo, Kevin and a few of the others, got involved in a few of the community projects. The damage wreaked by the storm had put an end to the differences between Antoine and Théo, the pupils from the school showed a great willingness to help the distressed families, often at the expense of their own. They were like an army of scouts.

In the end, unable to bear it any longer, Antoine slipped away and took the path up to Saint-Eustache.

In the municipal forest, hundreds of trees had been toppled. Those directly in the path of the cyclone had been cleanly felled, leaving a series of eerily straight paths through the forest.

At Saint-Eustache itself, the damage was even more spectacular. The tangle was so thick it was impossible to penetrate, the forest seemed to have been completely levelled, the trees lay in a twisted heap. The one or two that had withstood the storm, for some unknown reason, seemed like lookout towers planted in a ravaged wasteland.

When he arrived home, Antoine was thoughtful.

Madame Courtin had dug an old transistor radio out of the attic and loaded it with batteries ransacked from various appliances around the house. She had her ear pressed to the crackling broadcast, as though she had gone back in time to the Occupation.

"Be quiet, Antoine, I'm trying to listen!"

The *capitaine* of the *gendarmerie* was insisting that the circumstances surrounding the disappearance of Rémi Desmedt "will continue to be rigorously investigated", but that the devastation suffered in the Beauval area was such that it would be impossible to carry out further searches. Forces across the *département* are actively pursuing lines of enquiry, etc. . . .

The impact of the storm on the local area was the subject of a "Special Report". In a brief interview, Monsieur Weiser said that he was devoting every effort to persuading lumber companies to come and harvest the hundreds of hectares of fallen trees in the municipal woodland so the timber would not go to waste.

Meanwhile, the land around Saint-Eustache, long the subject of legal wranglings between numerous heirs – to say nothing of others who could not be traced – was of no significant market value and would be left in its current state.

Antoine went upstairs to his room. Rémi was dead, gone for ever.

It was over.

Rémi Desmedt had become a memory, and would remain so for a long time to come. Sometime in the distant future, when the forest of Saint-Eustache was redeveloped, there would be little left to find of the child's remains.

And by then, Antoine would be long gone.

Because from that moment his mind was focused on a single plan: he would leave Beauval.

And he would never come back.

2011

15

Time wrought no changes in Madame Courtin's sense of propriety. From an early age, Antoine had learned that to defy her was as fatiguing as it was futile. Alright, he agreed, he would come home for Monsieur Lemercier's party – I'll be there by seven o'clock latest, promise. The only concession he managed to extract from her was that he would not have to stay long; as far as his mother was concerned, the fact that he still had to study for exams was an unimpeachable alibi.

While waiting for Laura to call, he had decided to take a short walk around Beauval. Without her he was quickly bored, he missed everything about her, her slender, sensuous arms, her sweet breath. He felt a longing to be with her . . . and a fierce desire to fuck her. Young, dark-haired, exhilarating and utterly uninhibited, for Laura desire and pleasure were as vital as food and oxygen. Intelligent and somewhat wild, she was capable of throwing herself headlong into all sorts of dubious situations, but she had a keen sense of integrity that got her out of trouble at the first sign of danger. This woman, who promised to be an exceptional doctor, was just as capable of dragging Antoine into wicked yet wonderful escapades. Life with Laura was a firework display, a myriad of pyrotechnical possibilities into which Antoine launched himself happily, passionately. Laura was the shining shore of his existence. There were times when he took pleasure in these moments when they were separated, in the mingled melancholy and anticipation. But there were others, like today, when being apart from her weighed on him and he felt terribly alone. From the very beginning, their relationship had been volatile, like Laura, whose notion of sexual relationships was that they were passionate, fleeting and wholly impermanent. And yet somehow it had lasted, and lasted still; they had been together for three years now. They had established that neither of them wanted children, which might seem rare in a young woman but perfectly suited Antoine: he could not imagine bearing the burden, the responsibility for a child's life, he was panicked at the very thought. Then Antoine, ever restless and eager to travel far away, confided that, when he finished his studies, he wanted to work with a humanitarian aid programme and Laura said she had been thinking the same thing. A relationship that had begun with wild and wanton sex was cemented by this shared goal. One day Laura had said, "From an administrative point of view, working in humanitarian aid, it would be more practical if we were married . . ." She said it casually, the way she might have mentioned something they needed to add to a shopping list, but once planted, the idea burrowed into Antoine's mind.

Now, the prospect of marrying Laura made him happy,

and the thought that it was she who had proposed restored his faith in himself.

He needed to buy batteries for his computer mouse. He decided to walk into town.

As he left his mother's he could not help but glance at the garden of what had once been the Desmedts' house. Now remodelled, almost rebuilt, it was home to a forty-something couple and their twin girls with whom Madame Courtin was polite but distant – after all, they weren't really from these parts.

After the storm, the Desmedts had been offered a council house in Abbesses, on the outskirts of Beauval. Amazingly, in early 2000, Monsieur Desmedt had been spared in the wave of redundancies necessitated by the state of Weiser's factory. Word had it that he had been kept on only out of pity. Monsieur Mouchotte spread vicious rumours about him at the time, but they stopped some months later when Monsieur Desmedt suffered a ruptured aneurysm and died in his sleep.

It had put years on Madame Desmedt, her face was deeply lined, she seemed utterly drained. Antoine occasionally bumped into her, she had put on weight and walked arthritically, as though she had spent her whole life working as a cleaner.

She and Antoine's mother were no longer friends. In fact, they both behaved as though there had been a falling-out, as though some secret, unpardonable incident had led to a parting of the ways. After Bernadette was rehoused in Abbesses, they rarely ran into each other except at the shops, and even then it was just hello and goodbye, the storm had swept away their neighbourly camaraderie. No-one really noticed, not even Madame Desmedt. In that period of turmoil and grief, many friendships had faltered and new and often unexpected bonds had been forged, the calamity visited on the town had profoundly unsettled relationships between its inhabitants. In the case of his mother and Madame Desmedt, Antoine obviously knew rather more than other people, but that period, rarely discussed now, was invariably dismissed by Madame Courtin as "the storm of '99", as though nothing of note had happened in Beauval beyond some fallen trees and a few damaged roofs.

For a long time she had worried, tirelessly watching local news bulletins, reading the newspaper every morning, things she had never done before. Then, gradually, her anxiety had faded, she turned off the television and cancelled her newspaper subscription.

Antoine took a right turn towards the town centre. He felt as he always did. He hated everything, their house, this street. He hated Beauval.

He had got out while still at school. His mother had been surprised when he said he wanted to go to boarding school. Now, even though he still came to see her, his visits were as brief and as infrequent as possible; in the days leading up to these trips he felt uneasy, and he was always finding new excuses to leave early.

In his day-to-day life he put it out of his mind. Rémi Desmedt's death was an old wound, a painful childhood memory, he would go for weeks without being troubled by it. Not that Antoine was indifferent; his crime simply ceased to exist. Then he would see a little boy in the street, or in a film; the mere sight of a *gendarme* triggered a nameless, uncontrollable dread. He would be overcome by a suffocating panic, a palpable sense of impending doom, and it required a superhuman effort to dispel the terror with slow deep breaths and positive reinforcement, constantly scanning every judder and lurch of his imagination as one might worriedly keep an eye on an engine that has suddenly overheated.

Truth be told, the terror never went away. It dozed, it slumbered, and it returned. Antoine lived with the knowledge that, sooner or later, this murder would catch him up and ruin his life. He was facing thirty years in prison, a sentence that would be halved because he had been a minor when the crime was committed, but even fifteen years was a life sentence since, afterwards, he would never have a normal life. A child murderer can never be a normal person, because it was impossible to think of a twelve-year-old murderer as normal.

The investigation had never officially been closed. He could not even count on the statute of limitations.

Sooner or later, a fearful storm would loom and, with a power born of its age, would lay waste to everything in its path, his life and the lives of his mother, his father, it would not be content merely to kill him, it would ensure that he went down in history, his name, his face, would be notorious, not a trace of the man he was now would survive, he would be the "child killer", the "killer child", the "schoolboy slayer", a new precedent for criminologists, a clinical case for child psychologists.

This was why, more than anything, he wanted to go far, far away. He knew that even on the far side of the world these images of Beauval would continue to haunt him, but he was relieved to think that at least he would not have to run into people who were closely or distantly caught up in his tragedy.

Laura would sometimes wake to find him sweating, feverish, frantic or, alternatively, brooding, bleary and desolate. She could not fathom the reasons for his unexpected panic attacks and there were times when she felt that Antoine's urge to work in humanitarian aid was questionable. And, being one of those women who cannot bring themselves to turn a blind eye, she often tried to raise the subject. To no avail. Antoine had never brought her to visit the place where he had grown up. When eventually he did, perhaps she would be able to talk to those closest to him, understand him, help him.

He had just arrived at the *mairie* when Laura called.

"So," she said, "how's your mother . . . ?"

Madame Courtin was unaware of Laura's existence. Antoine's curious, irrational secrets had annoyed Laura for a time, but she was not the sort to attach too much importance to social niceties. She liked to joke about it precisely because it made Antoine uncomfortable.

"I hope she's not angry that I didn't come . . ."

This time, Antoine was not embarrassed. Instead he was aroused by Laura, he had always found sex to be a powerful anxiolytic. He began to murmur to her, crude, urgent whispers that left her speechless. He talked as though he were lying on top of her and she had her eyes closed. Then he would pause, leaving long silences that dripped with desire as he listened to her staccato breathing.

"Are you still there?" she said.

The silence suddenly felt different. Antoine was no longer thinking about her, he was somewhere else, she could sense it.

"Antoine?"

"Yeah, I'm still here . . ."

His tone said otherwise.

He was accustomed to seeing the photograph of Rémi Desmedt in the right-hand corner of Monsieur Lemercier's shop window, yellowed by the passing years. The boy's disappearance still cropped up in conversation, an unsolved mystery never truly faded, but the posters appealing for witnesses had long since been bleached by sunlight, and as they disappeared they were not replaced; these days the only ones remaining were in the police station, pinned up with a dozen other missing persons, and here, in the window of Monsieur Lemercier's shop.

"Antoine?"

The poster had moved. It was no longer in the corner where it had always been, it was now in the centre. And it was no longer the old photograph with its washed-out colours but a vivid, recent print.

Next to the child with the carefully slicked hair, wearing a yellow T-shirt with a blue elephant, was a teenager who looked eerily like the little boy. Age-progression software had imagined a seventeen-year-old Rémi Desmedt.

"Antoine!"

The poster no longer described the clothes he had worn at the time, nor the date when he disappeared – Thursday, December 23, 1999. Antoine saw his ghostly reflection superimposed over the face of this teenager he had never known, whom he alone knew did not exist. Everyone in Beauval nurtured the hope that little Rémi was still alive, that he had grown up and forgotten the boy he had once been, but it was an illusion, a lie.

He thought about Madame Desmedt. Did she have a copy of the poster on her sideboard? Did she wake every morning and look at the child she undoubtedly still loved, and at this young man she had never met? Did she still believe that she would one day see him alive again, or had she given up?

Antoine finally answered Laura, but the tension between them was broken. He walked on, he felt nervous, his earlier arousal replaced by a vague dread. Yeah, I'm here, he was saying to her, but he longed to get into his car, to drive away.

"When do you get back?" Laura said.

"Soon . . . day after tomorrow . . . Maybe tomorrow, I'm not sure."

He wanted to say: I'm leaving now.

He abandoned his walk and headed home, where he went up to his room to study, but still the poster perturbed him, he felt threatened. And yet, short of someone discovering the body, he could not imagine any possible threat. Although the investigation had never officially been closed, no-one was actively searching for Rémi Desmedt. It was completely irrational, but he felt as though the threat was in the town itself and existed only when he came back here.

Two or three times over the years, he had forced himself to walk up to Saint-Eustache. The place was exactly as the storm had left it twelve years earlier; the trees piled in a tangled heap had begun to rot, it was almost impossible to reach the centre of the forest. Being a doctor, he knew all too well what the remains of Rémi Desmedt would look like a decade on . . .

Then, suddenly, the computer-generated image in Monsieur Lemercier's shop window had somehow brought the dead boy back to life, made him as real, as present as he was in Antoine's nightmares. What had changed over the years – and this saddened Antoine – was not the knowledge that he was condemned never to speak about this to anyone, but the realisation that his priorities had changed, that the little boy he had killed was no longer the most important thing in his life. All his efforts, all his energy was now focused on himself, on his ambitions, on his safety. It had been some time since he had woken with a start and pictured little Rémi's limp hands before him, since he had heard the boy's plaintive cries for help. The central character in this tragedy was no longer the victim, but the killer.

Before he realised, it was 7.30 p.m. He could not decently arrive any later; he set off for the party.

Monsieur Lemercier was celebrating his sixtieth birthday. It was late June, the weather balmy, almost summery. A barbecue in the garden, music, bunting, the usual paraphernalia, the air smelled of grilled meat, there were little barrels of red and white wine. They ate from paper plates that collapsed, with plastic knives that cut nothing.

In Beauval, life ticked on like the workings of a clock. Time in the town that had once been shaken by disaster and mystery had resumed its peaceful, almost imperceptible flow. Ten years on, the people Antoine had once known had barely changed, and were steadily being replaced by a younger generation that – minor details aside – was much the same.

"It's a lovely spread, don't you think?"

Madame Courtin did a few hours' cleaning for Monsieur Lemercier every week. A very decent man, she would say, very respectable. In her language this meant that, unlike Monsieur Kowalski (for whom she had not worked in many years, and whom she never mentioned), he paid her what he owed on time.

Antoine shook hands with various people, accepted a glass of wine, then a second, ate something from the barbecue. At his mother's urging, he stopped to congratulate Monsieur Lemercier and to thank him for the invitation.

Plastic champagne flute in hand, Madame Courtin was chatting to Madame Mouchotte. The events that had distanced her from Bernadette Desmedt had brought her closer to Émilie's mother, that stunningly beautiful woman with a harsh face, who spent half her life in church and the other half cleaning her house. When business at the Weiser factory eventually picked up, Monsieur Mouchotte had been offered his job back, but this long spell of unemployment had left him embittered, a bitterness that was etched on his face, he scowled at everything. Much of his resentment was focused on Monsieur Weiser – his arch-enemy when he had been made redundant and his saviour on the day he was rehired – whom he thought symptomatic of everything that was wrong with the world. He had accepted his old job at the Weiser factory with grave satisfaction, like a man who, after a long and terrible injustice, had finally been restored to his rightful place. He had always needed someone he could hate, and for a long time it had been Monsieur Desmedt. Now that he was dead, Monsieur Weiser had been promoted to the highest rank of those Monsieur Mouchotte despised. Keeping as much distance between them as Monsieur Lemercier's garden would allow, the two men spent the evening cordially ignoring one another. Even at the factory, when he needed to issue instructions, Monsieur Weiser never referred to Monsieur Mouchotte by name, only as "the foreman".

To Antoine, Mouchotte's wife remained a mystery, a paradox. A sanctimonious old prig trapped in the body of a model, she spoke little and seldom smiled, which gave her the air of a prima donna, an ice maiden, though Antoine saw it as a form of hysteria.

"Hello, Docteur . . ."

"Hi, Doc!"

Émilie, blonde and smiling, held her champagne flute delicately like a fruit. Théo had just finished eating a sausage and was licking his fingers. Antoine had not seen them in a long time. He kissed Émilie. Théo clumsily wiped his hand on a napkin and proffered it. Ripped jeans, tailored jacket, pointed brogues, everything about his outfit screamed that he did not belong in this backwater, that he belonged to a different species. He took the three glasses and drifted off to have them refilled.

Alone with Émilie, Antoine felt self-conscious, she still had a certain way of looking at him.

"What do you mean, 'a certain way'?" she said, intrigued.

Antoine would have found it difficult to explain. She always seemed on the point of asking him a question. Or surprised by what he had said, by who he was.

Over time, Émilie had grown to be more and more like her mother, to whom she was still passionately devoted – no-one in her eyes ranked higher. And it was hardly surprising that they should be so much alike. Beauval was a town where children grew up to be their parents and expected to take their place.

They chatted a little about the party. Antoine asked what she had been up to. She was working at a branch of Crédit Agricole in Marmont.

"Engaged," she said, showing off her ring exultantly.

Oh, yes, Beauval was a town where people still got engaged.

"Théo?" he asked.

Émilie burst out laughing and quickly clapped her hand over her mouth.

"No!" she said, "Me and Théo? No way!"

"I don't know . . ." Antoine stammered, a little piqued that she had thought his question so preposterous.

She flashed the ring again.

"Jérôme is a sergeant in the army. He's currently posted to

New Caledonia, but he's just waiting for his transfer, he'll be back in France in September and we'll get married then."

Antoine felt strangely jealous, not that she had a man in her life, but that it had never been him. Even when they were at school they had never gone out, he felt he had missed every opportunity, that she had never thought of him as attractive, simply as someone she hung out with because they had known each other for ever; it irritated him to remember how much she had haunted his teenage fantasies. He had been obsessed with her blonde hair. He blushed.

"What about you?"

"Much the same . . . I still have to finish my residency, but after that we're going away . . . To work in humanitarian aid."

Émilie nodded gravely. Humanitarian aid was good. It was obvious from her expression that the concept had no real meaning for her, but the moral connotation commanded her respect. The conversation was over. What else was there to say? Between them, there were as many things unsaid as there were memories. They looked at the garden, at the little crowd laughing and shouting, the smoking barbecue, the music blaring from the speakers lined up beside the house where, beneath the new layer of paint on the render, it was still possible to make out the old high-water mark from the flood.

Théo reappeared with the plastic glasses and the three of them continued with their small talk. In a flash Antoine saw them again, standing on the steps of the church before Midnight Mass long ago. He remembered the brawl when he found out that Théo had been spreading rumours . . .

He took a sip of wine and looked away.

In Beauval, everything reminded him of Christmas 1999. What had happened then belonged to another life, even Beauval had moved on, but since the mystery of little Rémi's disappearance had never been solved, there were still embers that could be rekindled by the slightest breath; whenever he found himself in a crowd like this, he felt threatened, every gesture was laden with significance, subject to interpretation, a source of fear . . .

"Antoine!"

It took him a moment to recognise Valentine, she looked as though she had put on a kilo for every year. She spun around, irritated, to some screaming brat, "I said *stop* that!" She gave a vicious wave as though trying to bat away a determined wasp. In her arms she cradled a baby munching on a handful of crisps. Her husband, a good-looking lad, built like a lumberjack but with a mouthful of rotten teeth, slipped a proprietorial arm around her shoulders.

Antoine went on shaking the outstretched hands, kissing the occasional guest. Théo seemed to be following him, as though he had something to say and was waiting for the opportunity. Their eyes met once or twice, and then finally Théo leaned towards him.

"I'm like you, these people bore me rigid."

"No, it's not that."

Théo gave a little laugh.

"Come off it . . . They're dumb as shit."

Antoine was embarrassed by Théo's attitude. He too felt

that he had little in common with this world, that he belonged to a different, more modern species, he found the town anti- quated, narrow-minded, stolid . . . he hated it, but he did not feel contempt. Théo always had been pompous, it was hardly surprising to hear him talking about Beauval with contempt. He was working on launching a start-up whose precise function was not entirely clear to Antoine, there was a lot of talk about *expert systems* and *networking capabilities*, Théo's vocabulary was sprinkled with English expressions that were meaningless to him. He did his best to look interested, like people with a poor grasp of a language who give up trying to understand and simply nod from time to time. Émilie came back to join them, but she did not listen – this was men's talk, it did not concern her.

Then they drifted off in different directions. Antoine carried on drinking. Probably a little too much, he realised, especially since he had never been able to hold his alcohol.

He had made a promise to his mother, and he had come; he had also warned her that he did not plan to stay, so it was time to leave.

It was impossible to say goodbye to everyone, he would have to be careful if he was to slip away without offending anyone. He poured himself another glass of wine, trying to look casual, and coolly strolled towards the gate – no-one was looking at him, he set the glass down on a table and went out, closing the gate behind him. Phew.

"Leaving already?"

Antoine started.

Émilie was sitting on the low wall, smoking a cigarette.

"Yeah, I mean, no . . ."

Émilie gave the bell-like laugh Antoine had been aware of earlier. It was one of her little tics. She punctuated conversations with this little laugh, and while it would seem charming if she did it once or twice, it soon became tiresome. It was as though she used it to replace words she did not know.

"Does everything make you laugh?"

He immediately regretted the question, but Émilie did not seem to notice the venom. She gave a vague wave that could have meant anything.

"Right, well, I'd better be off," Antoine said.

"I'm heading home too."

They set off together.

Émilie lit another cigarette, and the smell of smoke, the cool night air and her delicate perfume mingled pleasantly. Antoine was almost tempted; though he had never enjoyed it, he had succumbed to the temptation twice or three times in his life. His earlier anxiety had dissipated, leaving only an intense weariness. A cigarette . . . why not?

Émilie returned to the conversation they had had earlier. She said she was intrigued by Antoine's plan to work in humanitarian aid. Why did he not want to be a . . . normal doctor? He could not summon the energy to give an honest answer, so Antoine was blunt.

"Being a family practitioner can get a bit boring."

Émilie nodded. There was something she did not understand.

"But if you find it boring, why did are you studying medicine?"

"No, it's not medicine itself that I find boring, it's just the thought of being a family doctor."

Émilie nodded again, but there was still something she did not quite get. Antoine stole a glance at her. My God, those high cheekbones, that mouth, the wisps of blonde, there, at the nape of her neck . . . The top buttons of her blouse were open and Antoine could see a hint of her firm breasts, he hung back slightly, letting her walk a little ahead so he could see the glorious curve of her arse . . .

"Because, I mean, being a doctor," she was saying, "It must be really interesting being able to cure people."

There was something profoundly sad about the fact that such a charming, sexy, young woman could be so fatuous. She spoke entirely in generalities, with ready-made ideas that required little or no thought on her part. She skipped about abruptly between subjects, most of them related to the only thing she truly knew: the people of Beauval. While Antoine studied her from head to foot, observing the perfection of certain details (her eyebrows, her ears – the girl even managed to have beautiful ears, it was absurd), Émilie had gone back to their childhood, to the time when they were neighbours, to shared memories . . .

"I've got loads of photos of us at school! And at the leisure centre . . . with Romane, Sébastien, Léa, Kevin . . . And Pauline!"

She was talking about people Antoine barely remembered but who she seemed still to know. As though this town and indeed her whole life was simply the school playground several years on.

"I should show them to you, you'll die laughing!"

That little laugh tinkled again in the darkness, charming, feminine, infuriating. What was it that she found so amusing?

For Antoine, school photographs evoked no fond memories. The image of Rémi Desmedt that had haunted his childhood had been a school photograph. It was a ritual, on the day of the school photograph you slicked down a stray lock of hair, you wore a clean shirt, as though heading to Sunday Mass.

"I'll send them to you if you like."

This idea seemed to thrill her so much that she paused for a moment. He gazed at her. That beautiful triangular face, those pale eyes, those soft lips . . .

"Yeah, sure . . . if you like," he said.

There was an awkward silence. Antoine looked away and they walked on.

Even in the town centre they could hear the distant echo of music from Monsieur Lemercier's garden. As they approached the *mairie*, desperate for something to talk about, Antoine mentioned the huge plane tree that had been brought down by the storm.

"Oh, yeah," Émilie said, "the tree."

She was silent for a few moments and the shadow of the plane tree eclipsed their conversation.

"That tree was kind of like the history of Beauval."

Antoine said nothing, what was there to say? There was

another silence. The warm June air, the hushed darkness, the wine, their unexpected encounter, this entrancing girl, everything was propitious to confidences, to revisiting questions he had been brooding over.

"What questions?" Émilie said, her tone naive and utterly without malice.

"Well . . . you and Théo for example . . . What happened between you?"

This time, Émilie's tinkling laugh had no effect.

"We were thirteen, for God's sake!"

She stopped in the middle of the street and turned to him in surprise.

"You're not going to get all jealous are you?"

"Yep."

He could not stop himself. Straightaway he regretted the answer, which was really an attempt to be funny. Because more than anything he blamed himself for having been a slave to her beauty and her charms for so long. And now he blamed her too, for being what she was.

"I was terribly in love with you."

It was a simple, sad statement. Émilie stumbled and grabbed his sleeve, but instantly she let go, as though the situation made her gesture inappropriate. Antoine felt as though he had done something wrong.

"Don't worry, I'm not declaring my undying love!"

"I know."

As they came to his house, Antoine remembered seeing Émilie's face at her bedroom window on the day of the storm.

"You looked so tired . . . And you were so pretty. You were really . . . beautiful."

This belated confidence made her smile.

She pushed open the gate, walked to the end of the garden and sat on the swing-seat which creaked softly. Antoine joined her. The seat was much narrower than it looked, or perhaps it was tilted slightly . . . Antoine felt Émilie's soft, warm hip pressed against him, he tried but failed to edge away.

Émilie gave a little push with her feet and they swung. A pale yellow light spilled from the streetlamp. Everything was silent, they did not say anything.

The movement of the swing pressed them closer together. Then Antoine did something he knew he should not do: he took Émilie's hand in his and she snuggled into him.

They kissed. From the first moment, it was a disaster.

He did not like the way she kissed, the avid probing of her tongue made him think of a dental examination, but he carried on because, in the end, it didn't matter as they did not love each other. That made everything more simple.

It was a harmless fling, a comfortable flirtation, the consequence of years spent in each other's company without ever touching. They could do this now precisely because they did not have to. They had been childhood friends. There was history between them, they needed to close the gap. To be sure. To have no regrets. The little girl he had been so in love with had nothing to do with the young woman in his arms who was stunning but stupid. And who, at this moment, he eagerly desired.

Everything about the situation was artificial, they both understood this, but they also knew that what they had started would carry on to its logical, inevitable conclusion.

Antoine slipped his hand into Émilie's blouse and cupped a warm, supple breast, she placed her hand on his crotch. They continued their awkward, irrepressible kiss, spittle trickled down their chins, they did not stop for fear of having to speak.

Antoine gave a stifled moan as his fingers found her warm and wet.

Her hand, as she grasped him, was like her lips: clumsy, single-minded, brusque.

They wriggled out of their clothes.

Émilie turned and placed her hands on the back of the swing-seat, legs parted slightly. In an instant, Antoine was inside her. She arched her back, encouraging him to go deeper, and bent her head so she could kiss him again, greedily, thrusting her tongue with the same eagerness. She gave a soft, animal whimper as she felt him tense and come inside her . . . He would never know whether she had come too.

They stayed pressed against each other, uncertain what to do, fearful of even looking at each other. Then they started to laugh. A remnant of their childhood came back to them, the impression that they had played a trick on the grown-ups, on life.

Antoine, all thumbs, pulled up his trousers, Émilie balanced precariously as she slipped on her underwear and smoothed down her dress.

She gave her little laugh, squeezed her knees together, hand on her belly like a child surprised at being taken short. She rolled her eyes and waved a hand up and down, fingers splayed, as though shaking off water, uh-oh, uh-oh . . .

She kissed Antoine – a quick peck on the lips – and then dashed off. When she got to the gate, she turned and blew him another kiss.

Even their parting was a fiasco.

Had his childhood not ended when he first came face to face with death, the day he killed Rémi, Antoine would have said that it ended that night.

He checked his mobile as he went indoors.

Laura had called four times but left no message. He punched in her number, but hung up immediately. Talking to her, which meant lying to her, was more than he could face. The evening had been a disaster, he could not understand how things could possibly have turned out as they had. Passion, maybe. But honestly, for all the passion he still felt for Émilie . . . He would have ended up in an argument.

He gave up on the idea of calling Laura, he would make some excuse . . . He would think of something.

His mother had kept his room for him, though the wallpaper and the furniture were new. His school desk, his chair, his old bed and almost everything else had been lovingly stowed away in the cellar, but a handful of objects had been spared this exile: a globe, a poster of Zidane, a rucksack, a pencil-case, his Megatron Transformer, a cushion emblazoned with the Union Jack – a curious selection whose logic Antoine had never deciphered.

He hated these things that brought him back to a time he

tried to keep at bay, but since he rarely came home, and since his mother had taken great pains to redecorate his room, he had neither the heart nor the energy to follow his instinct to toss everything into a box and leave it out on the pavement.

His mobile vibrated. Laura again. It was almost one o'clock in the morning. He felt ill at ease in this time, in this room, in this place, in this life, he could not summon the courage to answer.

When the mobile finally stopped throbbing, he breathed once more, and heard voices out in the street. His mother was coming home with the Mouchottes. What would have happened had he and Émilie been caught shagging on the swing-seat like a couple of teenagers?

It was too late now to get into bed and feign sleep. He sat at the table so it looked as though he were working. It was ridiculous and humiliating to engage in such pretence, but what else could he do?

Having noticed the light on in his bedroom, his mother came upstairs.

"You shouldn't work so late, darling, you need your beauty sleep!"

The phrase she had said over and over down the years, one that masked her pride at having a hard-working son, a successful son. She walked across the room and opened the windows in order to close the shutters, then she stopped, suddenly struck by a thought.

"I meant to say, you know they're planning to redevelop Saint-Eustache?"

Antoine felt a shudder run down his spine.

"How do you mean 'redevelop' . . . ? Redevelop what?"

Madame Courtin turned back to the window.

"Well, they finally tracked down all the heirs. The *mairie* has bought the land and they're planning on building an amusement park for children. To listen to them, there'll be kids flocking to it from all over the *département*. Me, I'm not convinced."

Faced with any proposal, any initiative, Madame Courtin always began by expressing serious misgivings.

"They say they've conducted surveys, that it'll appeal to families, that it'll create local jobs. We'll see. Right, time you got some sleep, Antoine."

"Who told you all this? About the park . . ."

"The plans have been posted in the *mairie* for a couple of months now, but what do you expect, you're never here, so you're hardly likely to know what's going on . . ."

The following morning, Antoine set off for his jog early. He had not slept a wink.

At the *mairie*, on the display board where official notices were posted, he pored over the press release announcing the development of the parc Saint-Eustache.

Work on clearing the site was to begin in September.

16

The holidays were a nightmare. He was wracked with worry. He had passed his exams, but he came through the ordeal utterly drained. He never wanted to set foot in Beauval again. It was irrational, since he would have to visit his mother sooner or later, but he made excuses, explaining that he was going on a long trip – though lack of funds meant that he and Laura only went away for a fortnight. The computer-generated image of a teenage Rémi Desmedt had been a shock, but the news that Saint-Eustache was to be redeveloped meant disaster, and he could not know how or when it would come. His mind dragged him back to the most harrowing period of his life, one which had come to entirely define his childhood. They would find the body. The investigation would be reopened. The police would re-question witnesses. He had been among the last people to see the boy alive, he would be called in. The theory that the child had been abducted by a passing stranger would be dismissed, the investigation would focus on Beauval, on the inhabitants, the family, the neighbours and, inevitably, the clues would lead them to him. It would all be over. Worn down by the last twelve years, he would not have the strength to lie.

Antoine spent the whole summer fantasising about running away. He researched places from which he could not be extradited. But deep down he knew he would not do it, he did not have the nature or the temperament to be a fugitive in a foreign country (even this romantic word was at odds with who he was). His life had always seemed to him to be narrow and restricted, he was not some ruthless, cynical, highly organised, career criminal, he was just an ordinary murderer who had been lucky until now.

He resigned himself to staying put, to waiting, and slipped into a morose, anguished acceptance.

Now that he was an adult, it was not the thought of prison that terrified him, but the ordeal: the trial, the newspapers, the television, the media swooping on Beauval, stalking his mother, the headlines, the interviews with experts, the articles by legal commentators, the photographers, the statements by neighbours . . . He pictured Émilie staring vacuously into the camera, she would not boast about their night together. The mayor would do his best to absolve the town of blame, but it would be futile: Beauval had nurtured both victim and killer, they had grown up barely a dozen metres apart. They would goad Madame Desmedt to tears so that they could film her, flanked by Valentine juggling her three little brats, and gravely pose the question, the sempiternal question: How is it possible for a twelve-year-old to become a murderer? Everyone would lap up the story since, compared to him, they would feel splendidly normal. Some television channel would broadcast a documentary about famous historical murder cases, going back as far as police records would allow. The Beauval murder would exorcise the violent urges of the whole populace, people could happily lay the blame on a single person and have the satisfaction of seeing that person punished for an act of which any one of them would have been capable.

In a few short minutes he would soar to the firmament of memorable murderers. He would cease to exist. Antoine Courtin would no longer be a person, he would become a brand name.

His mind was in turmoil, whirling with terrifying images, then abruptly Antoine came back to earth and realised that for the past half hour he had not spoken, or listened or responded to Laura's questions.

They lived in a little apartment in an area some distance from the university campus, but close to the teaching hospital.

If their three years together had been a wild, never-ending sexual odyssey, since Antoine's return from Beauval in June they had barely had physical contact. Laura did not give up easily, and Antoine played along with various little games in which his virility was not required. Although she was frustrated, Laura waited for things to improve. The Antoine she knew had never been particularly cheerful; he was quiet and secretive, grave and apprehensive, and this was precisely what she loved about him. He was moodily handsome – happiness simply made him dull. His gravitas gave those around him a feeling of solidity brutally undermined by his sudden panic attacks. And lately, his anxiety had escalated to a worrying degree. Laura assumed there were problems with his family. Or perhaps he was beginning to question his vocation as a doctor? Eventually she was drawn to a hypothesis that was as likely as it seemed impossible: Antoine was seeing another woman.

For Laura, jealousy required an energy that she simply could not summon. In desperation, she fell back on a psychiatric explanation, which was all the more reassuring for a doctor: if she could not address the root causes of the problem, medication would tackle the symptoms.

She was preparing to raise the subject with him when she discovered, quite by chance, that Antoine was already taking a daily dose of tranquillisers.

July and August passed.

Madame Courtin was worried that Antoine had not been to see her since June. She kept a mental record of his visits and could reel off the exact dates he had been to Beauval over the past five years. Curiously, she did not complain to him, she merely noted that he came less frequently, as though his estrangement was the result of a tacit agreement that was regrettable but necessary.

Several times a week, when it hit him that work was soon to begin on the amusement park at Saint-Eustache, Antoine was transported back to his last day in Beauval, to those wretched, worthless hours, to the image of the teenage Rémi, to the party he would not have attended but for his mother's insistence, to the foolish moments spent with Émilie.

The reasons for what happened between them remained a mystery. He had wanted to possess her because she was attractive and as a sop to his childhood obsession, it was a small measure of desire and a larger one of revenge. But what about her, what had she wanted? Had she wanted him, or something else? Had she simply played along? No – she had been a willing participant, he remembered her pervasive tongue, her hand, the way she had turned, had arched her back, the way she looked into his eyes at the moment he entered her.

At this distance, he was still torn in his feelings for the woman. In his mind, her beauty, which rated very highly on his scale of values, was inextricably linked with the depressing inanity of her conversation. He remembered her childish enthusiasm when she had talked about her old photographs.

The most inconsequential ideas clearly remained lodged in her memory, because in mid-September, in a telephone call with his mother, Madame Courtin mentioned that Émilie had come by to ask for his address.

"She wants to send you something, she didn't say what."

This thing about the photographs kept playing on his mind.

He imagined opening the envelope, and in his dreams his own face was superimposed with that of Rémi at six and Rémi at seventeen, and the morphed image looked like the ghostly faces on the headstones of children who have died too young.

He thought about the sideboard in the Desmedts' house, about the space left by the missing photo frame that seemed to be waiting for justice to be done.

He resolved that, when the photographs arrived, he would

throw them away without even opening the envelope. It was not as though he would need to explain himself, in the years he had been visiting Beauval he had barely seen Émilie, and now, fortunately, his visits were even more infrequent . . .

Late September.

This was when Émilie made her appearance, not in the form of an envelope of photographs but as Émilie herself, in the flesh, wearing a print dress that was frankly ridiculous but did nothing to hide her beauty. Carefully made up, perfumed and styled as though for a wedding, she was radiant as she rang the doorbell. Laura opened, Hello, I'm Émilie, I've come to see Antoine.

For Laura, it was a revelation.

The visitor did not need to say another word, Laura turned, Antoine, it's for you! Laura grabbed her jacket, slipped on her shoes and by the time Antoine, shocked by this unexpected visit, tried to react – Wait! – she had disappeared, her panicked footsteps echoing on the stairs. Antoine leaned into the stair-well, called her name, saw her hand sliding along the banister to the ground floor. He wondered where she had gone and felt a sudden pang of jealousy, then he turned, remembering the reason for her flight.

He stalked angrily into the apartment.

Émilie did not seem in the least embarrassed.

"Mind if I sit down?" she said.

Then, to justify the request, she added:

"I'm pregnant."

The blood drained from Antoine's face. Émilie talked for a

long time about "their night together", it was horribly embar-
rassing. She described their poignant reunion, the sudden,
almost visceral surge of desire they had felt and, for her at least,
"pleasure unlike anything she had ever known . . ." She could
not speak for Antoine, "but me, well, I haven't slept a wink
since that night, I fell in love with you all over again the moment
I saw you, I think I've always been in love with you, even if
I didn't want to admit it to myself," etc. Antoine could not
believe his ears. The situation was so preposterous that, had he
not suspected the potential consequences and the implications
of her performance, he would have laughed.

"It was just . . ."

He stopped, fumbling for words. The doctor in him was
screaming something he did not want to say aloud. He had to
force himself to ask:

"But who's to say . . . that I was the one who . . . ? Well, you
know what I mean . . ."

Émilie had a little couplet prepared. She set her handbag
down at her feet and crossed her legs.

"I can hardly be pregnant by my . . . well, by Jérôme. He's
been away for the past four months."

"But you could be pregnant by someone else!"

"Yeah, that's right, why don't you just call me a slut while
you're at it?"

Émilie was shocked by his remark, she had obviously never
imagined that such a question might arise. Antoine was forced
to apologise:

"That's not what I was trying . . ."

He stopped and calculated, and was staggered by the result: it had been thirteen weeks since what Émilie had insisted on calling "our night together".

Bluntly, a legal termination was impossible.

Everything was suddenly clear: she had waited until it was out of the question before coming to seek him out.

"Of course I did, Antoine! I don't want an abortion, it's just not right. Besides, my parents . . ."

"I don't give a damn about your parents."

"Well I do, and I'm the one who's pregnant!"

Antoine wondered how much it would take to change her mind. Could he pay her off?

"And you're the father," she said, lowering her eyes in a gesture learned from the television.

"I don't get it, Émilie, what is it that you want?"

"I've told my . . . I've told Jérôme I'm leaving him. I didn't tell him the whole story, I don't want him to think badly of us, but it's done."

"What do you *want*?"

She knit her immaculate blonde eyebrows, surprised that Antoine could ask such a stupid question.

"I want my baby to live. That's not too much to ask, is it? I want him to have every opportunity in life."

He squeezed his eyes shut.

"We have to get married, Antoine, my parents . . ."

Antoine leapt from his chair, incandescent, and roared.

"It's not going to happen!"

He had scared her, she shrank back in her chair. He

desperately needed to convince her that the idea was absurd. He tried to calm her, he went to where she was sitting, crouched down and took her hands in his.

"It's impossible, Émilie, I don't love you, I can't marry you."

He needed to come up with reasons she would understand.

"I could never make you happy, don't you understand?"

This argument left Émilie doubtful. She did not really understand what he was trying to say. The fact was, for two months she had been living with the idea that Antoine would "make things official", she had never considered any other possibility.

"You can still have a termination," Antoine insisted. "I'll pay for everything, don't worry. I'll get the money somewhere, I'll look for a good clinic, I'll take care of everything, but you've got to get rid of this baby because I'm not going to marry you."

"You're asking me to commit a crime!"

Émilie brought a tremulous hand to her breast.

There was a long silence.

Antoine had begun to despise her.

"Did you do it on purpose?" he said coldly.

"Why would I do that? And besides, how could I possibly ..."

Émilie was struggling with this simple idea, she did not quite know how to explain it, but she sounded sincere.

Antoine was devastated: it had been an accident. Émilie would have preferred to marry her *sergent-chef*, but in the meantime there had been "their night together" and, as disastrous as it had been, the results were here before him, Émilie was going to have a baby and Antoine was the father.

He was in denial. He got to his feet.

"I'm sorry, Émilie, but no. I don't want anything to do with this baby. I don't want you, I don't want any of this. I'll find the money, but I don't want a child, not now, not ever, I just can't do it, I don't expect you to understand."

By now the young woman was on the brink of tears. He had an image of Émilie going home with the news. It was hard to imagine her coming here without extensively preparing for the discussion with her parents, with her saintly mother. He could picture them from here, the whole Mouchotte tribe, the father, stiff and upright as an Easter candle, the mother wrapped in her mohair shawl . . . How could they have imagined that Antoine would give in, would marry their daughter? It was incredible.

Things were not going as Émilie had anticipated. Now it was her turn to get to her feet and come closer to Antoine.

She wrapped her arms around his neck and, before he had time to react, pressed her lips to his, snaked her tongue into his mouth and waited for Antoine to respond (even she must have questioned the purpose of this ritual, and if she did not feel anything, she did it with conviction, indeed with passion, but with no thought, no plan, no skill).

Antoine turned his face to one side, loosened her arms and slowly backed away.

Stung by this rejection, Émilie dissolved into tears. The weeping girl was terrifyingly beautiful, and for a moment Antoine faltered. But mentally he had lashed himself to the mast so he could resist the Sirens' song, it took only a moment of envisaging the life that she was planning for him to summon a strength that was impervious to everything. He gently laid a hand on her shoulder.

A few minutes earlier, he had hated her, now he felt sorry for her.

A fleeting thought occurred to him – who knew about this besides the Mouchottes? He was not thinking about himself, because he had no intention of ever going back to Beauval, he was thinking about his mother. It was all so sad.

"You're forsaking us?" Émilie said.

She had a real knack for coming out with melodramatic clichés, where did she find them? She blew her nose loudly.

"I can't do what you want, Émilie, I'm sorry. I'll take care of everything: I'll find a good clinic, I'll pay whatever it costs, no-one need ever know, I promise. You're young, I'm sure you'll have lots of babies with Jérôme, you can have a family with him, but not with me. But you have to make up your mind fast, Émilie . . . otherwise I won't be able to help you."

Émilie nodded. She had come here with a plan and it had failed. She had said the words she had prepared, she did not see what more she could do. Forlornly, she got to her feet.

For an instant, it occurred to Antoine that she took a certain pleasure in this situation that allowed her to play a role: she was heartbroken, a tragedy was being played out, she was the heroine – it was just like television.

She left a manila envelope on the table. The photographs of the class. My God, she had brought them with her . . .

Had she imagined that they would snuggle together on the

bed, laughing as they leafed through them. That Antoine – captivated, enthralled, enamoured – would lay a hand on her swelling belly and ask if the baby was kicking yet? He was stunned by her naivety.

After she left, he sat for a long moment and considered the consequences. He felt a glimmer of hope: until now, almost miraculously, he had made it unscathed through every crisis, through every trap that life had put in his path. When he was certain Rémi's body would be found, no-one had found it, he had slipped through the net; despite the fact that she was pregnant, Émilie had gone away empty-handed . . . He began to believe that his luck might continue. He thought about luck for the first time in an age. He felt a great weight lift from him.

He waited for Laura with unexpected calm.

She came back a very different woman to the one who had left.

"You could have opened the windows, it stinks like a tart's boudoir in here!"

That said, she grabbed her backpack and began stuffing things into it at random.

Antoine smiled; never had he felt more sure of himself. He took her by the shoulders and, smiling, forced her to turn around.

"O.K., fine, once – *once* – I slept with an old classmate who means nothing to me. She came here to try and stir things up, I threw her out. I love you."

Antoine was convincing because everything he was saying

was true, he had told no lies, except perhaps by omission, and that, in this moment, did not matter.

He felt suddenly invincible, he radiated such power that even Laura was startled. Still smiling, Antoine forced her to drop the clothes she was holding.

Deftly, firmly, he peeled off her sweater, and swept along by a wave of desire they fell back onto the bed, rolled onto the floor, and rolled over and over until they hit the leg of the table. Antoine was already inside her, Laura was not quite sure how he had managed it, her whole body began to tremble, a delicious shudder that came in waves, coursing from the soles of her feet, lifting her off the floor, arching her back, and she cried out. Twice.

And fell into a swoon.

17

Émilie wrote letters. Two, three times a week. Laura would set them on the table with a weary sigh. Antoine read them, at least at first. Crudely cobbled together, they were sprawling, barely intelligible screeds, but the broad message was always the same: "Don't desert me and our baby". Emilie's handwriting was childlike (she dotted her i's with little circles), she strung together melodramatic clichés intended to show the depths of despair to which Antoine had reduced her. Phrases like "surely you can't abandon your own flesh and blood" were followed by references to the "fire you have kindled in me", to the "waves of desire" that "engulfed" her, references to "that night" that had left her "shattered with pleasure". The mediocrity of her writing was almost painful, it was clear what kind of woman she was.

But though the letters were fatuous, her despair was entirely genuine. Unable to have a termination because of her parents' religious beliefs (and perhaps her own), she was destined to become what in Beauval they still called an "unmarried mother", forced to raise her child alone. He tried to imagine what her life would be like. His imaginings were not exactly noble: beautiful as she was, he thought, even with a kid she would manage to bag herself a husband. As for her parents, they would be thrilled to have this cross to bear, they would carry it with martyred dignity and everyone would be happy.

In early November, as rain set in all over France, Antoine slipped in the road as he was running for a tram, and narrowly managed to stop himself falling.

A few days later, his mother was not so fortunate. While crossing the main street in Beauval, she was hit by a car. With a muffled thud, Madame Courtin was lifted off the ground and landed heavily on the pavement. She was rushed to hospital from where the staff contacted her son.

Antoine and Laura were in bed (for the past month, they had spent most of their time here – almost breaking up can work wonders in a relationship . . .). Antoine picked up the telephone and froze. Laura held her breath. The nurse would not be pressed on details, but insisted that it would be best if he came as soon as possible.

Shaken by the news, Antoine took the first possible train to Saint-Hilaire, arriving late that evening. Even if visiting hours were over, the nurse had said, they would let him in to see her. He took a taxi. At the hospital he was greeted with such delicacy that he had to interrupt to say, "It's O.K., I'm a doctor."

The on-call doctor was not taken in: he was dealing with a patient's relative, nothing more or less.

"Your mother has sustained a serious head injury. Clinical examinations have revealed no fracture and the C.T. scan looks positive, but she is in a coma . . . I can't tell you much more at this point."

He did not allow Antoine to study the scans, and offered only essential information. He behaved exactly as Antoine would have done in his position.

Madame Courtin looked as though she were asleep. Antoine sat next to the bed, took his mother's hand in his and began to sob.

Laura, meanwhile, had booked a room for him in Saint-Hilaire.

L'Hôtel du Centre.

He arrived in the early hours. The lobby reeked of wax polish, something he had not smelled since his childhood, as though it were a characteristic scent of the region. Flock wallpaper, floral drapes, candlewick bedspread . . . Laura had chosen well: the room was just like his mother.

He lay down fully dressed and fell asleep. At some point he thought he woke, he did not know what time it was, and his mother was there, sitting on the edge of his bed.

"Antoine, is something wrong?" she was asking. "Sleeping there fully clothed, with your shoes on and everything . . . It's not like you . . . If you're not feeling well, why don't you just tell me?"

He shook himself awake, then took a shower, the pipes shuddered and rumbled and probably woke everyone in the hotel.

He called Laura, waking her, and her first words were I love you, her voice thick with sleep, I love you, I'm here, and Antoine looked around him, all he wanted was to curl up next to her, to breathe in her love, feel her warmth, melt into her, disappear, I love you, she said, her voice deep, distant and yet present and Antoine began to cry and soon after went back to sleep. But at first light he was up and out, walking through the streets, heading towards the hospital.

He wondered whether he should get in touch with his father. It made no sense, his parents had been divorced for so long. His father would either feel obliged to come in order to prove that he was close to his son, which would be a sham, or he would refuse because for more than twenty years this woman had meant nothing to him. There was no-one Antoine could call except Laura. It was strange how there were so few people in his life.

Madame Courtin's condition had not changed since the previous night.

Antoine read the patient notes, studied the graphs, instinctively checked the settings on the life-support machines. Then, having exhausted all possible distractions, he sat down next to his mother's bed once more.

One worry had superseded another. It was only now, in the silence of this hospital room, in his enforced idleness, that he realised he was only a few kilometres from Beauval.

It was impossible to know how things would turn out. Would his mother die? Would Rémi's body finally be discovered? And if so, would it happen before or after she passed away?

What Antoine found exhausting was not the guilt, nor the fear of being caught, it was the waiting. The uncertainty. The feeling that until he got as far from here as possible, anything might happen, his life could be ruined in an instant. It was only a matter of months now. Like a long-distance runner, it was those last few kilometres that seemed impossible.

In the early afternoon, Docteur Dieulafoy made a discreet, unobtrusive appearance. He always looked as though he had got the wrong room, as though he would turn and leave when he realised his mistake. This was probably what he intended to do when he saw Antoine in the room. Swiftly he masked his embarrassment, but only after that flicker of hesitation that so often betrays people who find themselves in unexpected situations.

Antoine had not seen the man in years. He looked much older, but his face, now deeply furrowed, was as impassive, as inscrutable as ever. Did he still live the same friendless, mysterious life, still spend every Sunday in a baggy tracksuit cleaning his surgery?

The two men shook hands and sat next to one another, silently watching Madame Courtin, then realised that their silence resembled post-mortem reverence.

"Where are you up to in your studies?" the doctor asked.

"Final year."

"Already?"

Docteur Dieulafoy's voice transported Antoine back to that curious moment half a lifetime ago: "If I'd admitted you to hospital . . . things would have been very different, you realise . . ."

It was true. If Antoine had been hospitalised after his attempted suicide, there would have been an investigation, he would have been questioned, he would have confessed to killing Rémi, his life would have been over, this was the fate the doctor had saved him from.

What exactly did he know? Nothing concrete. But a few hours after the disappearance of a neighbour's child, with the whole town agonising over the tragedy, a twelve-year-old boy's attempt to end his own life took on a terrible significance and presented him with a real moral dilemma.

"I mean, if something happens," the doctor had said, "you can come to me, you can call me . . ."

That day had never come. It was curious that the doctor should reappear now, when Antoine felt closer than he ever had to the abyss.

That "something" was about to happen, though Docteur Dieulafoy did not yet know it: the body of Rémi Desmedt was about to be discovered.

Antoine looked at his mother's ashen face.

She, too, had known there was "something", but she had chosen not to find out what it was. Intuitively, she had realised that her son was probably involved in the tragedy, she had done everything possible to protect him from some nameless but insistent threat, and this web of lies, half-truths and silence had held firm for almost twelve years.

Now Antoine found himself in a hospital room with the only two witnesses to his involvement, two people who, in their own ways, had chosen to remain silent.

The wheel was coming full circle.

At this very moment, flatbed trucks were carrying cranes up the hill towards the woods at Saint-Eustache, bulldozers were clearing away the fallen trees. The remains of Rémi Desmedt would not be scattered, nor buried beneath the heavy caterpillar treads of machines, they would rise up, like the statue of the Commendatore to demand that justice be done and that Antoine Courtin be apprehended, arrested, tried and sentenced.

Madame Courtin began to mutter something unintelligible.

From opposite sides of the bed, the two men looked at her, listened to the gurgling noises and struggled in vain to find some meaning in them.

"What are you planning to do afterwards?" the doctor asked.

What was he talking about? Antoine frantically racked his brain, then remembered their interrupted conversation.

"Oh . . . humanitarian aid. I passed the interviews . . . Well, that's the plan, at least."

Docteur Dieulafoy was thoughtful for a moment.

"I see, you want to get away."

He looked up and stared at Antoine, as though struck by a sudden revelation.

"It's very parochial here, isn't it?"

Antoine tried to protest.

"Oh, but it is," the doctor interrupted him. "It's a small town. I do understand, you know. What I mean is . . ."

He trailed off into a long pensive silence and then got to his feet and left as he had come, like a cat, quiet and anonymous, taking his leave of Antoine with a curt nod and a surprising and enigmatic remark:

"I'm very fond of you, Antoine."

Antoine's fantasy of never again setting foot in Beauval did not even last the day: in the late afternoon, the hospital administration requested Madame Courtin's papers and effects, Antoine would have to go and fetch them, there was no-one else.

The prospect of returning to Beauval was overwhelming. His mother lived next door to the Mouchottes, and he had no trouble imagining the mortifying scene he would face if Émilie noticed his presence.

He played for time, found all manner of excuses, he would wait until after his mother had been bathed, he would leave after the consultant's visit . . .

Without thinking, he flicked on the television to watch the evening news.

The lead story on every national news channel was the same: that morning, the bones of a small child had just been unearthed in the woods near Saint-Eustache.

The *gendarmerie* offered a guarded statement confirming the discovery and refused to speculate on the possible identity of the victim, but for the reporters and for those who lived in the *département* there was only one possibility: it had to be the body of Rémi Desmedt. Who else could it be?

Antoine had been waiting for this news. He had had more than ten years to steel himself for it, but in the end, as with the death of a loved one, he was not really prepared.

The reports kept coming, relegating all other news stories to the background. There was footage of the building site, the stationary trucks, the silent bulldozers, the crime-scene examiners from the *Identité judiciaire* in their white papery suits surrounded by police cars whose whirling blue lights strobed the cordon of barricades where there was a milling crowd of uniformed *gendarmes* and plain-clothes officers, but all this was merely set dressing, all the media really cared about was Rémi Desmedt. In the hours that followed the discovery, the photograph that had long ago featured on MISSING posters, appeared on every television screen and was seen by almost everyone in France. Reporters had rushed to find Madame Desmedt and laid siege to the apartment block in which she lived. Though they had not yet managed to interview her, they had no trouble getting statements from neighbours, shopkeepers, town councillors, passers-by, postmen, teachers, parents – everyone was moved to tears, the whole town seemed to relish the thought of being united in grief.

Everything that Antoine had rationally attempted to imagine was swept away by the ravages of this media feeding frenzy. Come on, think about it, what is going to happen . . .

It was at this moment that Laura decided to call. Antoine did not have the courage to answer.

While Madame Courtin continued to rave, her voice growing louder, Antoine spent the rest of the day glued to the television, following every new development, listening to theories about the disinterred remains, the identity of the victim (again, that photograph of Rémi smiling, hair neatly combed, dressed in the yellow T-shirt with the blue elephant), to speculation about the possible cause of death and the abuse the child might have suffered pre- or post-mortem. There were calls to reopen an investigation that the police, the judiciary and the ministry for justice insisted had never been closed. Calmly, confidently, people waited for officers to find a clue that would open up a new lead, and arrest the guilty party at last.

Antoine felt queasy as he watched a young woman, her face a mask of affected grief, hand clutching a microphone emblazoned with a news channel logo, reporting from the steps of the *mairie* surrounded by a solemn, mournful crowd who jostled subtly to get their faces into the shot.

"According to investigators, the theory that the child was abducted remains plausible, however, it seems clear that the boy was not taken far, and may have been kept prisoner in the immediate vicinity, in which case the inquiry will focus on the town itself . . . On Beauval, from where I am currently reporting."

The tragic drama had come home, the serpent slithering towards the Courtin household. Antoine might well be questioned, the boy he had once been might be asked whether he remembered anything. Each new lie would be another gruelling weight to lift, he simply did not have the strength any longer.

When the *gendarme* came to the door, Antoine would without a word hold out his hands to be cuffed.

He had forgotten he was supposed to go to Beauval to pick up his mother's papers. Although Madame Courtin was by now increasingly delirious and her ravings had grown more shrill, Antoine was so exhausted that he dozed off in the chair next to her bed; by the time he woke, it was five in the morning. Seeing himself in the bathroom mirror, he looked like a fugitive from justice. He left the hospital, walked as far as the station, found a line of taxis waiting for the first train from Paris and asked to be driven to Beauval, hoping he would get to his mother's house without encountering anyone. And he did.

As he got out of the taxi, he could not help but steal a glance at the house next door. By intuition or sheer chance, though it was not yet six o'clock, Madame Mouchotte, frozen, ageless, was standing at the window watching his every move. Her spectral beauty evoked something from a nightmare, it was like seeing a spider in her web, ready to pounce . . .

He hurried indoors.

Madame Courtin's house was spick and span as a parochial pin. Her papers had been kept in the same drawer since the beginning of time. The heavy, restless nap in the hospital chair had left his body stiff and aching. He lay down on the sofa and drifted off, only to wake in the late morning, dog-tired and depressed, as addle-brained as if he had spent the night on a drunken binge or at a Christmas party.

He fired up his mother's ancient appliance to make himself a coffee with that same smell, the same taste he remembered from his childhood.

Unable to resist the temptation to pick up where he had left off, he turned on the television. The face of the state prosecutor immediately filled the screen, discussing, "the identity of the victim whose remains were discovered yesterday".

"Forensic investigations have confirmed that the body is that of Rémi Desmedt, who disappeared on December 23, 1999."

Antoine dropped his cup and it shattered on the floor. His first reaction was to glance towards the window, as though he expected to see the entire populace of Beauval gathered outside the old Desmedt house, to hear the crowd baying for revenge.

"The rising floodwaters of 1999 did not reach the hills of Saint-Eustache and the fact that the boy's remains had been protected by the numerous trees brought down by the storm allowed officers from the *Identité judiciaire* to perform a D.N.A. analysis."

Antoine stared at the shards of the china cup, the pool of coffee spreading slowly, like a wine stain across a linen table-cloth . . .

"There is evidence that the boy suffered a blow to the right temple, probably the cause of his death. It is too early to state whether he suffered any other injuries."

Though it was illogical, Antoine was terrified that the investigation was already beginning to point to him. A panic that was exacerbated by the past two days, which had left him shattered and exhausted . . .

He got to his feet, clumsily gathered together the papers he needed to take to the hospital, called the taxi company in Fuzelières and went outside to wait. He desperately needed air.

He did not have time to turn back before being buttonholed by a radio reporter at the garden gate.

"Were you living in the house next to Rémi Desmedt at the time of his disappearance? Did you know him well, what sort of a boy was he . . . ?"

Antoine stammered a few words which the reporter asked him to repeat.

"He was . . . uh . . . he was my neighbour . . ."

Antoine was hopeless: didn't he understand they were looking for something more personal, more emotional? The reporter sounded frustrated.

"Yes, yes, of course . . . but what was he like, as a boy?"

The taxi pulled up and Antoine jumped in.

Through the rear window he saw that the reporter had already turned her attention to a young blonde woman. It was Émilie, stepping out of her house, wrapped in her mother's shawl. She had filled out. As she answered the reporter's question, she glared resentfully at the departing taxi.

Madame Courtin was still suffering from bouts of delirium, she tossed and turned, thrashing her head this way and that, muttering a few garbled words over and over, and now and then a name (Antoine! Christian!), her son and her ex-husband, and other names (Andrée!) that probably dated back to her childhood.

Antoine spent the whole day by her bedside, wiping her forehead, stepping outside when the nurses bathed her only to come back and slump into the chair again, shattered, sickened and distraught.

Madame Courtin's ravings were like an endless loop, her

head twitching in the same manner, her lips repeatedly forming the same sounds (Antoine! Andrée!). Staying with her was all the more distressing since he had to listen to endless reports about the "Rémi Desmedt case" from the television mounted high on the opposite wall.

The newsrooms had unearthed archive footage. Though barely twelve years had passed, the images seemed from so terribly long ago: Beauval with the plane tree still standing in the main square; Rémi's house and Monsieur Desmedt bellowing at reporters, trying to shoo them like a noxious swarm of flies; the mayor, Monsieur Weiser, bustling self-importantly on the morning of the search, the rescue parties setting off for the woods, then footage of the storm, the flood, the battered cars, the fallen trees, the weary, hopeless townspeople . . .

Laura spent all day sending Antoine text messages, all of them amounting to the same thing: I love you.

Madame Courtin began to emerge from her coma at about 6.00 p.m. Antoine shouted for the nurses. There was much upheaval and commotion, he was ushered out and waited nervously in the corridor. It was more than an hour before a nurse came to let him know that his mother had regained consciousness, she told him that they planned to keep her in for observation for several days, that he did not need to wait around, they would keep him informed of any developments.

He went into the room to gather up his clothes, he would go back to the hotel to sleep, sleep . . .

The television was still on. Antoine looked up at the screen. "Officers from the *Identité judiciaire* have identified a hair on the body that does not belong to the victim. It is impossible to say with any certainty that the hair was left by the killer, though it remains a strong possibility . . . Forensic technicians are currently working to create a D.N.A. profile. Once they have a result – which could be very soon – it will be compared to those held on the National D.N.A. Database. If a match is found, the police will almost certainly call on the individual concerned to come forward and explain the presence of the hair on the remains of the dead child . . ."

18

Shortly before midnight, as Antoine was lying on the bed in his hotel room, he heard footsteps in the corridor and a knock on his door. Without waiting for a response, Laura came in, set her bag down and tossed her jacket onto a chair. Antoine did not have time to say a word before Laura was lying on top of him, her faced pressed into the crook of his neck, breathing hard as though she had been running. Antoine wrapped his arms around her. He did not know quite how he felt about her unexpected presence.

At any other time, he would already have rolled her over, but not tonight . . .

He could not begin to imagine how Laura would react when she found out the kind of man he really was. With his mother it was different, she had always known there was something. Laura would leave, his mother would die of shame. Having lain on top of him for a long time, Laura got up and undressed, then undressed him as though he were a child, lifted the sheets and they slid into bed, she snuggled close to him and fell asleep.

Though Antoine was utterly worn out, sleep still would not come. Laura's breathing was deep and peaceful. He felt saddened by her unconditional trust. Softly, quietly, he began to cry.

Without opening her eyes, without shifting her position, Laura traced his cheek with her finger, wiping away a tear, then cupped his face with her hand.

Moments later he was asleep, and by the time he woke up it was daylight, his watch read 9.30 a.m. Laura had gone, leaving a scribbled note in the margin of a page torn from a magazine: I love you.

In the two days that followed, Madame Courtin's recovery progressed in leaps and bounds. Though she was still pale and drawn and ate little, her speech now was only occasionally garbled, her sense of space and time returned, her balance improved and – after a final round of X-rays – doctors were planning to allow her to go home.

Doubtless to prove that she "still had all her marbles", Madame Courtin insisted on packing her suitcase herself, steadying herself on the nightstand or the bed when her balance faltered.

As Antoine passed her clothes, she folded them neatly and carefully packed them into the case, but both of them were glued to the television screen where all talk was of new developments in the "Rémi Desmedt case".

Antoine recognised the young female reporter he had seen outside Beauval's *mairie* some days earlier.

"The D.N.A. results are in, and police now know a little

more about the individual whose hair was found with the remains of Rémi Desmedt. D.N.A. profiling confirms that the individual in question is a male Caucasian, and while it is impossible to speculate as to his height, they can also confirm that he has fair hair and brown eyes. Such characteristics are common, and there is insufficient information to develop an E-Fit of the individual."

Antoine waited until he had listened to this information several times before drawing a conclusion he could not quite bring himself to believe: the police had a D.N.A. sample, very probably his, but he did not appear in the police database, and as long as that remained the case, the chances of his being convicted of the murder of Rémi Desmedt were almost nil . . .

It seemed unlikely that the investigation would be reopened. After all, what other leads did they have? More than a decade after the event, the Rémi Desmedt case would make a few ripples and then fade away once more.

Would Antoine be able to pick up the pieces and carry on with his life?

"Well, now, Madame Courtin, we'd been counting on you staying with us for Christmas!"

The short, dark-haired nurse with the twinkling eyes probably made the same joke to every patient when they were discharged, and she was expecting the usual reaction. Instead she was greeted by two people sitting stock-still, staring at the television, and eventually she too turned to look.

The camera was trained on the supermarket in Fuzelières,

on the side door reserved for staff only, as Monsieur Kowalski emerged flanked by two *gendarmes*.

"The lone suspect in the case remains one Monsieur Kowalski, the former owner of a charcuterie in Marmont, who was arrested at the time of the disappearance but later released for lack of evidence. It seems highly likely that detectives will compel the witness to provide a D.N.A. sample which may then be compared to that found on the victim."

Madame Courtin seemed suddenly more agitated. She found it difficult to hide the anger that Antoine had always observed when it came to her former employer, as though she felt betrayed by this man. She had never made any secret of the fact that she thought him a skinflint and a slave-driver. She probably also felt the same bitter outrage anyone would feel on discovering that they have unwittingly rubbed shoulders with someone who later turns out to be depraved, devious, perhaps even a monster.

Antoine watched as Monsieur Kowalski was arrested for the second time, and for the second time he sensed, nebulously and with little shame, just how relieved he would feel if there were to be a miscarriage of justice. Not that it was a possibility this time: After all, D.N.A. could not lie, but still he felt a surge of hope that Monsieur Kowalski might be convicted in his stead. Antoine had not seen the man in years. He too had aged considerably, his hair was white and his gaunt face looked even more emaciated, he walked slowly, arms dangling limply.

His business had not survive his arrest in 1999. Trade in charcuterie had steadily declined, he had been forced to sell up and to take a job managing the meat counter of the super-market in Fuzelières.

Monsieur Kowalski would be released in a couple of hours, in a couple of days at most, it would probably be the last development in a case that would shortly be filed away in the police archives. With each passing minute, Antoine felt the weight on his chest lift, a whirl of images flashed through his mind: Laura, finishing their studies, going abroad together . . .

Madame Courtin and he went home ("A taxi! We could just as easily have taken the bus . . ."), she threw open the windows to air the house ("Really, Antoine, you might have thought to do it when you were here!"), wrote out a shopping list ("Mind you get Heudebert *biscottes*, if they don't have Heudebert, don't get anything!") . . .

The little frustrations Antoine had always found difficult to bear would soon be a thing of the past, but for now, he happily put up with his mother's fussing and fretting, so relieved was he to see her back at home. "There was more fright than hurt in it," she said to friends and acquaintances who telephoned. News of her return had already done the rounds in Beauval.

Antoine put off going into town for as long as he could to avoid being accosted by people asking for news of his mother. So Blanche is home, then? Oh, that's good, that's good, a terrible scare she gave us, you know, not that I was there myself, but I heard about the accident, dreadful, gave us all a terrible scare . . . He also wondered anxiously whether the Mouchottes had gone public with the news of their daughter's "condition", but no, no-one seemed to know. Neither Émilie nor her parents had been keen to acknowledge a situation they would have condemned in anyone else.

Théo, who was taking the *mairie* steps four at a time, gave him a little wave. He also ran into Mademoiselle, as Maître Vallenère's daughter was known. Twice a week, pushed by an orderly, she would leave the nursing home where she had lived since her father's death and take a tour of the town. She would sit for while on the terrace of the Café de Paris. In summer, she ordered ice cream, and the orderly wiped the drips from her chin, in winter she had hot chocolate which she drank in small sips. Though the outlandish multicoloured wheelchair was gone, she herself had not changed, she was as painfully thin as ever, her cold pale hands lay on the tartan rug and her eyes still blazed in a face that looked like a death mask.

In every shop he visited, Antoine patiently waited his turn as idle gossip was exchanged.

He was filled with a faint euphoria which, unsurprisingly, owed much to the exhaustion of recent days but which brought with it a feeling of reassurance. Were it not for this problem with Émilie Mouchotte . . . But even that was a minor embarrassment compared to the threats he had been facing. It might cost him a little money, big deal . . .

Still he could not believe it.

He would finish his residency, leave all this far behind, rebuild his life.

19

Two days later, to no-one's surprise, Monsieur Kowalski was released without charge, though he was still guilty in the eyes of the people of Beauval, who were slow to change their minds, no smoke without fire, they would never change.

As Antoine's fears gradually subsided, so too did his mother's interest in local news. She no longer sat glued to the television as she had during her time in hospital. Unlike Antoine, she barely listened to statements made by the *procureur de la République* from the steps of the district courthouse in response to questions from reporters.

"No, it is simply not realistic to subject the population of Beauval to mass D.N.A. screening. There simply would not be funds available for such a screening, but, more importantly, it would not be based on any clear evidence. We have no reason to assume that the individual whose D.N.A. was found at the scene (if indeed he is the man who murdered Rémi Desmedt) is a resident of Beauval rather than one of the neighbouring towns, or just someone who was passing through . . ."

"There you have it," Madame Courtin muttered, as though the state prosecutor had just confirmed a theory she had been defending all along.

With this last obstacle out of the way, Antoine was now free to leave: Madame Courtin was her old self again, it was time to go back and prepare for his final exams.

"Already?" said Madame Courtin, who could hardly believe it herself.

His mother, who insisted on organising a "little lunch" ("little" was the word she used for anything she deemed important), slipped on her coat and headed into town to be greeted like Lazarus returned from the dead, all the while maintaining an air of false modesty that made Antoine smile.

He packed up his things, poured himself a glass of port. They ate lunch, talking about nothing in particular, slightly stunned to find themselves here together when only two days ago the outcome of the situation had seemed far from certain.

Then Madame Courtin looked up at the clock and stifled a yawn.

"You've got time," Antoine said.

She went upstairs to have a little nap before his departure.

The house thrummed with silence.

Then the doorbell rang. Antoine opened it. It was Monsieur Mouchotte.

The two men did not shake hands, both embarrassed by this unseemly situation. Antoine realised that he had never actually had a conversation with Émilie's father. He stood aside and ushered the man in.

Monsieur Mouchotte was a tall man with hair close-cropped like a soldier's and an aquiline nose. This, together with his stiff bearing and his insistence on maintaining his dignity at all costs, made him look something like a Roman emperor. Or a schoolmaster from another century. In any case, he kept his hands clasped behind his back, making it easier to throw out his chest and keep his chin up.

Antoine felt ill at ease, he had no desire to sit through a lecture in morality, this whole situation was an accident. If the Mouchottes were determined that Émilie should have this baby, there was nothing Antoine could do about it, he had no reason to feel guilty, but it was clear from Monsieur Mouchotte's steely, almost threatening manner that he would not get off so lightly: they wanted money, they had probably worked out what a doctor was likely to earn.

Antoine clenched his fists, they would try and take advantage of the situation, he had not even thought to look up his rights.

"Antoine," Monsieur Mouchotte began. "My daughter succumbed to your advances. To your insistence . . ."

"I didn't rape her!"

Instinctively, Antoine realised that an aggressive stance that admitted no guilt was the most effective strategy, he had no intention of being duped.

"I never suggested that you did!" Monsieur Mouchotte protested.

"Just as well. I proposed a solution to Émilie, one that she rejected. That is her choice, of course, but it is also her responsibility."

Monsieur Mouchotte was speechless.

"Surely you're not suggesting . . ." He choked on the words, unable to say them aloud.

Antoine wondered whether Émilie had told her father that he had suggested she have a termination, or whether he had only discovered it now.

"Yes. That's exactly what I'm suggesting . . . In fact, it's still possible. It's borderline, but it's possible."

"Life is a sacred gift, Antoine! God has willed that—"

"Spare me the sanctimonious bullshit!"

It was as if he had slapped the man. For all his Roman airs, he was already out of his depth, something that only served to fuel Antoine's belligerence.

Drawn by the sound of her son shouting, Madame Courtin's footsteps now echoed on the stairs.

"Antoine?" she said as she reached the bottom step.

He did not turn around. As she leaned over the banister, Madame Courtin was greeted by the strange sight of two men facing off like fighting cocks, hackles raised, ready to come to blows . . . She tiptoed back to her room. Monsieur Mouchotte, puffed up with righteous indignation, had not even noticed her presence.

"How dare you . . . you have brought disgrace on my daughter!"

He was speaking in a deep bass register, enunciating each syllable to make it clear that he could hardly believe his ears.

"Oh," Antoine said, "if we're going to talk about 'disgrace', I wasn't the first, I can assure you."

Now Monsieur Mouchotte was incandescent.

"How *dare* you insult my daughter!"

The conversation was one-sided, and Antoine did not like to kick a man who was down, but he was not about to lower his guard. He decided to press his advantage.

"Your daughter is entitled to do what she wants with her body, it's no business of mine. But I don't—"

"She was engaged to be *married*!"

"Yes, she was, but that didn't stop her having sex with me."

Antoine needed to put an end to this situation at any cost, and with Monsieur Mouchotte there was little point in trying to be subtle.

"Listen, Monsieur, I can understand why you might feel embarrassed, but let's face it, man to man, your daughter wasn't born yesterday. Now she's got herself knocked up by somebody, but I'm no more to blame in all this than . . . well, well, let's say 'the others.'"

"I always thought you were a despicable young man . . ."

"Well, next time maybe you should tell your daughter to be more careful in her choice of lovers."

Monsieur Mouchotte nodded vehemently: Alright, O.K., fine . . .

"If that's how you want to play it . . ."

He whipped a rolled-up newspaper from behind his back and waved it about like a flyswatter. The local paper. Antoine could not tell whether it was today's edition.

"Everyone knows . . . these days, they can do tests."

"What are you talking about . . . ?"

Antoine was suddenly pale.

Monsieur Mouchotte realised that at last he was moving in the right direction.

"I'm going to press charges."

Antoine sensed the looming threat but could not grasp the repercussions it would have on his life.

"I'm going to sue you and force you to give a D.N.A. sample that will prove beyond doubt that you're the father of the child my daughter is carrying."

Antoine was dumbfounded, he stood open-mouthed, unable to think clearly.

This idiot was making threats without even considering the consequences.

"Fuck off," Antoine hissed in a toneless voice.

"It's not too late for you choose the path of righteousness over that of infamy," Monsieur Mouchotte said with finality, "as much for your sake as for Émilie's. Because let me tell you, I shall not be swayed in this. I will go to court, I will insist you submit to this test, and whether you like it or not, you will be forced to marry my daughter and to acknowledge this child."

He turned on his heel like an officer, slamming the door as he left.

Antoine needed to steady himself, he clung to the doorframe. He needed to find some way to counter this.

He raced up the stairs and into his bedroom, locked the door and began to pace up and down.

Would he really have to marry Émilie Mouchotte?

The prospect made him feel sick. Besides, where would they

live? Émilie would never agree to move abroad, to leave her parents.

More to the point, what chance was there that a humanitarian organisation would take him on if he was father to a toddler?

Would he be condemned to stay in Beauval?

It was unthinkable.

Antoine tried to imagine the situation in concrete terms. Monsieur Mouchotte would file a lawsuit. He would go to court, only to be told his grievance was preposterous. "This is something that is only enforced in cases of rape, Monsieur Mouchotte. Has your daughter made a complaint of sexual assault . . . ?"

No, Antoine reassured himself, no judge would countenance such a request, it was impossible.

But at the same time the judge would surely wonder why, if he was so convinced he was not the father, Antoine Courtin was not prepared to submit to such a test.

The judge would be puzzled by this man who refused to take a D.N.A. test at precisely the moment when investigators had released a D.N.A. profile of Rémi Desmedt's killer. More curious still, this same man had been one of the last people to see the child alive . . .

And so, just to be sure, Antoine would be taken in for questioning.

And he knew that he would never survive an interrogation about the events of twelve years ago. It was hopeless. He would try to lie, only to get bogged down and become flustered, the examining magistrate would find this suspicious – it would not be the first time a murder suspect had been arrested because of some trivial, unrelated offence . . .

He might even go so far as to order Antoine to submit to a D.N.A. test.

Better to give in.

Better to get the test over with, to put an end to his misgivings.

He felt comforted by this idea. After all, if it turned out that he was the father, he would simply pay Émilie child maintenance and that would be that! There would be no question of him throwing his life away by marrying that – that . . . He groped for a word but could not find one.

From the next room he heard muffled sounds, hushed noises, like a considerate guest in a hotel room where the walls are paper-thin.

His mother, as usual, was trying to pretend that nothing had happened by tidying her already-immaculate bedroom, something Antoine remembered from his childhood.

To hear her, to feel her almost physical presence, chilled him to the bone . . . If it emerged that he was the father – the guilty party, in other words – and that he had refused to marry Émilie, the Mouchottes would spread the news all over town, point the finger at the Courtin family . . .

What effect would that have on his mother's life?

It would be a stain on her reputation. Everyone would think of her as the mother of a coward incapable of facing up to his responsibilities, his obligations. She would not endure the knowing looks, the pointed remarks, the moral disapproval, it was beyond her.

Antoine had no-one but his mother, and she had no-one but him.

He could not put her through such a terrible ordeal.

It would kill her.

There was only one solution: take the test and hope that he was not the father. It was a long shot.

But there was another issue.

The news reporter's words echoed in Antoine's head: ". . . a D.N.A. sample which may then be compared to that found on the tragic victim."

The room started to spin and he had to sit down. If he agreed to a paternity test, the results – whether positive or negative – would have to be stored somewhere.

There would be a file on him. For a long, long time. Where were such results stored? Which departments had access to the database?

He could not be certain that, one day, they might not be compared to . . . the D.N.A. sample from Rémi Desmedt's killer.

At any moment, a government decree could authorise the police to cross-reference all available D.N.A. databases.

There would forever be a sword of Damocles over his head.

And so the only solution was to refuse to take the test.

Antoine was back where he had started. It was Catch-22: whether or not he took the test, the outcome would be the same.

What did not happen today would still be a threat tomorrow.

And for the rest of his life.

"What time is your train, Antoine . . . ?"

Antoine had not noticed his mother pop her head around the door. She could tell at once that her son was in a state.

"Never mind, you can always get a later one."

She closed the door and went downstairs.

Antoine paced up and down, trying to gather his thoughts, but again and again he had to face the facts. There was only one way out: he had to stop Monsieur Mouchotte from making a formal complaint.

Otherwise he would have to live in fear for the rest of his life, and even then he might end up spending fifteen years in prison, face a trial that would be a media circus, the grim fate of a child-killer . . . Everything he had so far managed to avoid.

Twelve years had passed since the crime he had committed when he was twelve years old, and the final act in the tragedy that had been set in motion in December 1999 might well be played out here, now . . .

Night fell.

He heard his mother going to bed, without a word, without a question.

He paced his room until morning. It was a grotesque situation. His whole life was one long, terrible defeat to which he had been doomed by a childhood catastrophe.

As dawn broke, he wondered whether, with Émilie, he had not in fact doomed himself. The sentence for his crime would not be years in prison, but a whole life from which he instinctively recoiled, a life that represented everything he despised, lived among nonentities, practising a profession he loved in circumstances he hated . . .

This was to be his punishment: to serve out his sentence as a free man, at the cost of his entire existence.

By morning, Antoine had accepted his defeat.

2015

20

It had been raining continually for more than a week. And now that the nights were drawing in, making house calls had become more and more wearing. Though he tried his best to be methodical, to map out a sensible route, he would get emergency calls while on his rounds, forcing him to go back to Marmont twice, and three times to Varennes, it happened again and again.

Antoine glanced at his watch: 6.15 p.m. There would be a dozen people in his waiting room already, he would be lucky to get home before nine o'clock. He caught sight of himself in the rear-view mirror. A few days before his wedding he had decided to grow a moustache, and he had kept it ever since. It made him look much older, even his mother said so, not that it mattered to him, or to Émilie. But then again, Émilie . . . She had always been a closed book. He had been very angry with her in the early days, and he blamed himself for being duped, for giving in to panic. He had even considered taking it, the D.N.A. test, but in the end he hadn't because it would not have changed the course his life had taken. It was too late for that.

So he let it go, and he saw his wife differently; he did not love her, but he understood her. She was a butterfly, unstable, volatile, subject to sudden flashes of anger with no forethought and no regrets. She was still immensely beautiful, she had recovered from her pregnancy within weeks, her belly was flat, her breasts flawless, and that perfect arse ... When he saw her in the shower he was still blown away. From time to time he would roll over onto her, and she always let him, she pretended to come, giving little muffled cries "because of the baby", then turn onto her side, telling him it was "even better than last time", and fall asleep. Antoine was convinced that Émilie had never had an orgasm. With anyone. He no longer fretted about their sexual relations, as a doctor he simply tried to ensure that she was careful, but it was a waste of time, she was beyond control.

In the early days, Antoine would feel a pang if he came home unannounced and saw Émilie appearing from the basement, smoothing her skirt and combing out her hair, and then bump into some red-faced electrician who had not even opened his toolbox. Had he been in love with her, it would have made him unhappy. In fact, he did feel a little sad, but not for himself. When he glanced at her surreptitiously, at the dinner table or in the kitchen, he felt a pang of regret to see such waste: this melancholy beauty who had nothing going on in her head.

Émilie accepted her life just as she put up with everything, from everyone. She had a penchant for fumbled trysts and fleeting quips.

Except with Théo. He had taken over the factory from his father two years earlier and replaced him as mayor at the last elections. Ever since, he had played the modern employer, the modish mayor, he attended council meetings in Diesel jeans, and ceremonies at the war memorial in an open-necked white shirt and no tie, he met with union leaders wearing Converse trainers. He feigned friendship, bitched about his salary, called everyone by their first name. And he fucked the doctor's wife – an old schoolfriend doesn't count.

Antoine came to a stop behind a timber lorry on the road near the outskirts of the forest. He had to wait. He dreaded these moments of quiet, in fact this was probably why he had come to love being a country doctor. Docteur Dieulafoy, whose practice he had bought a year earlier, had warned him: "Either you won't stick it more than two months, or you'll be doing it all your life, there's no middle ground." It was true. He had thrown himself into his work, he would probably never relax.

Otherwise, life had settled into a routine.

Émilie still trotted out the same pathetic clichés all day long, his father-in-law was proud that his daughter was now the local doctor's wife. The baby was monopolised by his in-laws because Antoine "had far too much work on his hands to be able to take care of him", which was true.

Little Maxime had been born on April 1. They had heard every possible joke on the subject, the whole family had one up their sleeve – I forgot his birthday. Ha! Ha! Only kidding, April fool! Calling the boy Maxime, a name that spoke volumes about the family's delusions of grandeur, had, of course, been a decision imposed by Monsieur Mouchotte.

After the wedding – which had been a complete nightmare: three months with four full-time organisers, family meetings to discuss the guest list, church meetings to rehearse the cere- mony, arguments over the menu, squabbles over the invita- tions, sheer hell – Émilie's pregnancy had rallied every last one of her relatives who all seemed convinced that she was the first woman to fall pregnant since the dawn of creation.

Émilie was a flamboyant mother-to-be. She proudly thrust out her belly as if it were the outward sign of inner bounty, she sailed past everyone in a queue with a triumphant smile, asked for a chair in every shop, she would breathe heavily until those around her began to worry, and then launch into a detailed description of the primary and secondary symptoms of her pregnancy, sparing no details, telling them about the pain, the diarrhoea, the morning sickness, the restless nights – I thought he was kicking, but no, it was just wind! Oh, the flatulence, it's because the abdomen is compressed, I tell you it's really something, the whole thing's gruelling (she loved the word gruelling), but it was also the "wondrous gift of life", and when she was in particularly good form, she would burble happily about how "giving birth to a child is the greatest adventure a woman can experience". Antoine was profoundly depressed.

At first, he had no feelings for his son, neither love nor hatred, the child was simply not a part of his life. Émilie and her mother were forever playing house with this baby he only occasionally encountered. He treated the child as he did most of the babies in the *département*, he was just one among many.

Then Maxime began to walk, he began to talk and, to his astonishment, Antoine realised that his son was nothing like the Mouchottes. At times he thought the boy took after him and felt flattered, even though this was something he had always found ridiculous in others.

Perhaps he noticed the resemblance because it was what he wanted to see. He stayed on the sidelines, he was content simply to observe. He did not yet know what their relationship held in store.

Antoine restarted his car and turned right, he was running more than an hour and a half late, the waiting room was probably heaving. Too bad, they would have to wait, in fact they were always happy to wait, Antoine had rapidly become a popular doctor among the people of Beauval. In his case, at least they knew his mother.

He parked at the foot of the steps, left the keys in the ignition, climbed out, drawing his coat up against the rain, and went into the huge house. He would not stay long, but he had promised he would come, so here he was. Good evening, Docteur, we'd almost given up hope of seeing you, here, let me take your coat, you know what she's like, she's very impatient.

Maybe. But she always pretended to be engrossed in something else. Every time he went into her room, she would look up in surprise, oh, it's you, what brings you here . . . ?

Mademoiselle was thirty-one now, but she looked fifteen years older. She was terrifyingly thin, but Antoine knew that her skeletal frame would probably defy death for decades to come. If Mademoiselle had ever longed to die, that desire had faded, like Antoine's dreams of running away.

He pulled up a chair, rummaged in his bag and, after looking around furtively, took out a bar of chocolate and slipped it under her blanket. The secrecy was merely a ruse, everyone knew Mademoiselle was not allowed chocolate, and everyone knew she ate it anyway, including her doctor, who was her principal supplier.

Mademoiselle lifted a corner of the blanket to look at the label and gave a little pout of disgust.

"You're a bad loser, Docteur . . ."

They had started playing chess when Antoine had taken over from Docteur Dieulafoy as attending physician at the nursing home, but he never had time to play a full game. Now they exchanged moves by e-mail, it had been her idea. Antoine would consider his strategy while driving to see a patient, send Mademoiselle his move before the visit, receive a response during the consultation and send his next move after he left. Mademoiselle was right, he was not a good loser. It was not the loss itself, but because it was systematic: he had never won a single game, and he brought a bar of chocolate every time he lost a match.

"I can't stay long, I'm running nearly two hours late."

"Oh well, your patients will just give up and go home, it might do them some good. When you visit them tomorrow you'll probably find they're all cured."

Always the same old story, like an old married couple.

Antoine clasped Mademoiselle's hand, her cold, bony fingers wrapped themselves eagerly around his, thank you, see you soon.

Driving back through the rain. Beauval.

The town had changed in recent years. The parc Saint-Eustache had been a roaring success. In peak season, visitors came from all over the region. Family-friendly, close at hand, the concept had proved a winner. Monsieur Weiser had helped the town to turn itself around, his son had been elected almost unopposed. Tourism created employment, the shop-keepers were happy and a town whose shopkeepers are content is a town that thrives.

This change of fortune coincided with the revival of the wooden toy market. What had been considered tacky in the 1990s was once again fashionable. As the French became more environmentally conscious, they suddenly discovered a love of train sets carved from solid ash and spinning tops whittled from pine trees. Employment levels at WEISER, WOODEN TOYS SINCE 1921, were almost as high as they had been before the financial crisis.

The waiting room was crowded and stiflingly hot, condensation was streaming down the windows.

Antoine cracked open a window, something no-one present had dared to do. He gave a general "Hello, hello", and a rueful shrug intended as an apology for his tardiness. There was a murmur of approval, people liked their doctor to be over-worked, it was a guarantee of his ability.

He recognised Monsieur Fremont, Valentine, Monsieur

Kowalski. Docteur Dieulafoy had greeted Antoine's proposal to take over the practice with enthusiasm. Antoine had been worried that, given the old doctor's passion for his job, he would be reluctant to retire, he might suggest they work together, interfere in every case, but his fears were unfounded. As soon as the surgery was sold, Docteur Dieulafoy moved to Viet Tri, a city to the north of Hanoi, to look after his mother, the eighty-year-old woman he had not seen in almost fifty years. Before he left, he had given Antoine detailed files on all of his patients and had even insisted on spending some considerable time talking through the more challenging cases.

It was at this point that Antoine discovered Monsieur Kowalski was registered with the practice, though he had not yet seen him in the surgery. With Valentine, he would have to reach a compromise. She would show up six times a year asking for a sick note, usually dragging several kids along so he would take pity on her. Antoine was very lax with her; though reluctant to write out a doctor's certificate, he always did so in the end. He did not admit it even to himself, but Valentine occupied a strange position in his life; he still thought of her first and foremost as the young girl devastated by her little brother's disappearance, the sister of the boy that Antoine had killed.

Antoine took his time preparing for the third part of his day, checking his equipment, ensuring everything was in order, slipping his wallet into the top drawer of his desk – the only one that locked – a reflex that owed more to magical thinking than to security, since a ten-year-old with a paper knife would have been able to prise it open in seconds. It was here that he kept Laura's response to the letter that he had sent her, a hurried screed written in a single sitting: Laura (not "my love", leave no room for misinterpretation), I'm leaving you (be simple, clear, decisive), a long explanation about Émilie, the only woman he had ever loved, whom he had got pregnant and was planning to marry, it's better this way, I'd only have made you unhappy, etc. The sort of moronic, mendacious, predictable letter that all cowardly men write to the women they finally decided to dump.

Laura's answer had come by return post, a large white sheet and, top left, the word "Fine".

He had folded it, slipped it into the drawer and locked it. And, over time, he had almost forgotten it was there.

Antoine wrote Valentine a sick note for one week, then ushered in Monsieur Kowalski, a lean man with a gentle voice and slow, deliberate movements. Antoine listened to his heart and, as he took his blood pressure, glanced down at the man's notes, oh yes, Monsieur Kowalski was a widower, he made a mental calculation, he would be sixty-six.

"Probably a virus . . ."

Monsieur Kowalski smiled and gave a fatalistic shrug. Antoine wrote out a prescription, as always he explained the medication and the dosages, he was careful to write legibly, to avoid being overbearing.

He set down the patient file, showed Monsieur Kowalski to the door and shook his hand.

Monsieur Fremont was already getting to his feet when,

on a sudden impulse, without taking the time to think, Antoine said:

"Monsieur Kowalski?"

All heads turned towards the door.

"Um . . . could you step inside again for a moment?"

He gave Monsieur Fremont an apologetic wave: If you don't mind, I won't be long . . .

"Come in, come in," he said, gesturing to the chair Monsieur Kowalski had just vacated, "sit down for a minute."

He stepped around the desk, picked up the patient file and flicked through it again.

Andriej Kowalski, born Gdynia, Poland, on October 26, 1949.

Antoine had one of those sudden intuitions that are so compelling that, at the time, they seem like an epiphany and which, a moment later, seem completely superficial.

But Monsieur Kowalski bowed his head and stared into his lap, and Antoine immediately sensed that he had been right.

For a long moment he said nothing, he did not know how to broach the subject . . . Because at any minute a door might open, and he did not know what was on the other side. And he did not know if he would be able to close it again. He was still holding the patient file. André.

"A few years ago my mother had an accident. She was in a coma for several days . . ." he began without looking up.

"I remember, I heard about it at the time, but she's better now, isn't she?"

"Oh yes, she's fine . . . In the hospital she was delirious . . .

She was calling out for people, my father, me . . . I was wondering . . ."

"'Yes?"

"I was wondering whether she called out for you. Your first name is André, isn't it?"

"I was christened Andriej, but here people say André."

Antoine might have been on the wrong track, but the question was nagging at him, so he felt he had to ask.

"And is that what my mother called you?"

Monsieur Kowalski was staring at Antoine and frowning. Would he fly into a rage, get up and storm out, or would he answer . . . ?

In a soft voice he said, "What are you getting at, Docteur Courtin?"

Antoine stood up, came around the desk and sat next to Monsieur Kowalski.

He had often met the man, had often stared at him because of the fearsome physique that, in Antoine as in many other people, inspired a sort of inexplicable awkwardness, but studying the man now he found he radiated the sort of tranquil power, that strength a young child often sees in his father.

Antoine's mind teemed with conflicting thoughts, he did not know how to move the conversation forward.

Monsieur Kowalski, for his part, did not seem at all troubled. On the contrary, he looked as though he would never say something he had decided to keep secret.

"If you don't want to talk to me . . ." Antoine said, "you're free to go. You don't owe me an explanation."

Monsieur Kowalski considered his decision for a moment.

"I retired last month, Docteur. I have a little house down south . . ." He gave a dry little laugh. "I call it a house, but that's dressing it up, in fact it's a caravan . . . but, well, it's mine. I don't think we're likely to run into each other again. I had planned to . . . I never thought that you'd ask me today, straight out, just like that."

Each phrase he spoke seemed taut, fragile, as though threaded onto a wire and likely to fall, to shatter.

"The reason I mention my retirement is, well . . . a lot of time has passed, these things don't really matter anymore."

"I understand."

Antoine put his hands on his thighs and made to stand up. But then he paused.

"You know, I was puzzled," Monsieur Kowalski said, "when I saw you that day in December."

Antoine stopped breathing.

"I was driving through the forest on the outskirts of Saint-Eustache, and then suddenly, in the rear-view mirror, I saw a boy dashing across the road, crouching in the hedge, the moment I saw him I knew it was you."

Antoine felt a mounting panic, a terror he had not felt in the four years since he had thought that he was safe, at last. Just when his life was sinking into a humdrum routine like quicksand, suddenly it all came flooding back, the death of Rémi Desmedt, the trek through the woods of Saint-Eustache with the child's body on his shoulders, the small, pale hands disappearing into the crevasse beneath the fallen beech tree . . .

He wiped sweat from his forehead.

He could see himself on the way back to Beauval, lying in the ditch, watching for cars before crossing the road.

"So I pulled up a little further on . . . I parked the van, got out and went back to see what was happening. I wondered if maybe you needed help. I didn't find you, obviously, you were long gone."

Monsieur Kowalski was the sole witness who could have steered the investigation towards Antoine in the immediate aftermath of Rémi's disappearance. Monsieur Kowalski, who had been arrested and persecuted at the time, and who, four years ago, when Rémi's remains were discovered, had been taken in again for questioning . . .

"But you—"

"I did it for your mother. I loved her very much, you see. She loved me too, I think . . ."

He bowed his head, his faced flushed, seemingly aware that the secret he had revealed was trite, almost banal.

"I'm sure you'll find this ridiculous coming from an old man like me . . . but she was the love of my life."

No, Antoine did not find it ridiculous, he too had had one great love in his life.

"I never admitted what I was doing that day because . . . we were together, the two of us. She was in the car with me. I didn't want to compromise her. She wanted our relationship to remain secret . . . and I had to respect that."

To avert suspicion, Madame Courtin had always been cold and distant towards him, offering snap judgements about

Monsieur Kowalski that in retrospect seemed terribly cruel.

Antoine struggled to piece things together. Monsieur Kowalski stops the car. What does his mother say?

Sitting in the car, she turns around but she sees nothing, she wonders what he is up to, she does not want to stay there, parked at the side of the road, she cannot afford to be seen with him . . .

Monsieur Kowalski gets out, he looks for Antoine, who he has just glimpsed running frantically towards Beauval, he doesn't find him, he gives up, gets back in the car and drives off . . .

What did they say to each other?

"I didn't say anything. It was a reflex, really, I had the impression that . . . how can I put this . . . that it wasn't the right thing to do."

This relationship between his mother and Monsieur Kowalski makes Antoine feel uncomfortable, though he struggles not to show it. Not because it was scandalous in itself, obviously, but people are always surprised and shocked at the thought that their parents could have a sex life – even when they are doctors. That was part of it, but there was something more ambiguous, more complicated, something that would take time and thought to work out, something that depended on the question: when had they first met?

Madame Courtin had started working for Monsieur Kowalski before Antoine was born . . . Two, three years before maybe. When had Antoine's father left? In his mind the dates, the years, the images were muddled, the ground seemed to be opening up.

Antoine suddenly felt sick.

He turned back to Monsieur Kowalski and saw that the man had got to his feet and was already at the door.

"None of this matters anymore, Docteur. You ask yourself a lot of questions, of course . . . I sometimes wondered . . . And then, one day, you stop."

This man who had suffered as much as he had was struggling to find the words to reassure him.

Antoine was shivering, as though he had gone out on a snowy day without a coat.

"Really, Docteur, don't worry . . ."

Antoine opened his mouth to say something, but Monsieur Kowalski had already gone.

Two days later he received a small parcel in the post. He opened it at his desk just before beginning his surgery.

It was his watch. With the fluorescent green strap.

It had stopped, obviously.

ACKNOWLEDGEMENTS

This novel would never have seen the light of day without the essential presence of Pascaline.

I would like to thank my friend Patrice Leconte (Saint Martin) for writing the letter that was needed precisely when it was needed. And on the subject of friends, how could I forget Jean-Daniel Baltassat (Saint Bernard) and Gérald Aubert, my fundamental friend . . . nor Samuel Tillie are to blame, but me alone. I would like to thank them for their help and their advice.

I recognise myself in the words of H.G. Wells, in his preface to *Apropos of Dolores*:

> *You take bits from this person and bits from that, from a friend you have known for a lifetime or from someone you overheard on a railway platform while waiting for a train or from some odd phrase or thing reported in a newspaper. That is the way fiction is made and there is no other way.*

And so, during the writing of this novel, certain images, certain expressions occurred to me that I knew came from elsewhere. Those I have been able to identify come from (in no particular order): Cynthia Fleury, Jean-Paul Sartre, Georges Simenon, Louis Guilloux, Virginie Despentes, Rosy & John, Thierry Dana, Henri Poincaré, David Vann, William McIllvaney, Marcel Proust, Yann Moix, Georges Simenon, Marc Dugain, K. O. Knausgård, William Gaddis, Nick Pizzolatto, Ludwig Lewisohn, Homer and doubtless several others . . .

PIERRE LEMAITRE was born in Paris in 1951. He worked for many years as a teacher of literature before becoming a novelist. He was awarded the Crime Writers' Association International Dagger, alongside Fred Vargas, for *Alex*, and was sole winner for *Camille* and *The Great Swindle*. In 2013, *The Great Swindle* won the Prix Goncourt, France's leading literary award.

FRANK WYNNE is an award-winning translator from French and Spanish. His previous translations include works by Virginie Despentes, Patrick Modiano and Michel Houellebecq.